WITHDRAWN
ANNE ARUNDEL COUNTY PUBLIC LIBRARY

That Witch!

Zoe Lynne

Harmony Ink

Published by
Harmony Ink Press
5032 Capital Circle SW
Ste 2, PMB# 279
Tallahassee, FL 32305-7886
USA
publisher@harmonyinkpress.com
http://harmonyinkpress.com

This is a work of fiction. Names, characters, places, and incidents either are the product of the author's imagination or are used fictitiously, and any resemblance to actual persons, living or dead, business establishments, events, or locales is entirely coincidental.

That Witch
Copyright © 2013 by Zoe Lynne

Cover art by Allison Cassatta
allisoncassatta@gmail.com

All rights reserved. No part of this book may be reproduced or transmitted in any form or by any means, electronic or mechanical, including photocopying, recording, or by any information storage and retrieval system without the written permission of the Publisher, except where permitted by law. To request permission and all other inquiries, contact Harmony Ink Press, 5032 Capital Circle SW, Ste 2, PMB# 279, Tallahassee, FL 32305-7886, USA.
publisher@harmonyinkpress.com

ISBN: 978-1-62380-692-7
Library Edition ISBN: 978-1-62380-927-0
Digital Edition ISBN: 978-1-62380-693-4

Printed in the United States of America
First Edition
May 2013

Library Edition
August 2013

This book is dedicated to the family, friends, and fans who have been so supportive.

Love and appreciation, in no particular order…

Alli—

I want to thank the kids of MAGY for giving me insight into the world of LGBT teens, and for taking me in and accepting me as one of their own.
Joe Cassatta and Jessica Murchie, for always being there and supporting me.
My friends and family, and the fans who have loyally supported all my crazy ideas.
Bia Tanos, thank you for taking that call back in October and wading into the insanity that is my mind.

Bia—

Tara France, for always being at my side even though we're thousands of miles apart. I luff you.
Spring Gardner for being my friend and guardian angel, as well as for never giving up on me.
Bertha Rayo and Marlene Rayo—thank you for being family without boundaries or conditions and for always accepting me for who I am.
Jagger Tanos, for being an amazing son and blessing me every day with laughter, happiness, and unconditional love.
Last but never least, Allison Cassatta for always believing in me, even when I didn't believe in myself. Love you, Brain!

We also want to thank the wonderful staff of Harmony Ink for giving our baby a home and bringing it to life. As always, you all have been a pleasure to work with.

Chapter 1

JEEZ, Brynn just wanted to hide in her corner of the lunchroom, away from the preppy-populars and the nerd-herds, the drama club geeks and the overachievers, and listen to the new Donnas album while she crammed for her calculus exam. But nooooo, her BFF, Miss-Nancy-Drew-Wannabe, kept nudging her arm every five minutes just to point out something Brynn really had, like, zero interest in. She played along, though, peeking through the cotton-candy-pink bangs covering her face to see what Laura wanted. This time it was Cassidy Rivers, and the queen of the in-crowd looked like she was on the prowl, with her bleached blonde clones loyally in tow, as always.

Brynn rolled her eyes and buried her head back in her book. She didn't care about Cassidy. The chick didn't even hit Brynn's radar, well... except for the fact she was probably the most gorgeous girl Brynn had ever seen. She had these startling steel-blue eyes and pouty pink lips, bright blonde hair that was obviously really hers because her perfectly shaped brows were about the same shade of blonde. Her cheeks were rosy and round, and when she smiled, the cutest dimples formed at the edges of her mouth.

Brynn mentally facepalmed herself. Was she seriously admiring Cassidy Rivers—of all freakin' people?

Maybe on some level she would've liked to have been accepted by Cassidy and the in-crowd. Those kids lived in the nicest houses and had the best cars. They shopped in all the swanky Majestic Hills shops, wore designer everything, and had the best life had to offer. Brynn had the means to fit in. She came from money like the rest of them, but those shops didn't appeal to her. Name brands didn't mean anything either. Her favorite boots came from an army thrift store. She listened to bands like My Chemical Romance and The Used, not Bruno Mars and Britney Spears. Still, it would've been nice to fit in, but there was no way she would admit that to anyone. No, it was totally more hardcore to pretend the preppy-popular kids were a vapid waste of space, and she could do soooo much better… with her *one* friend.

One earbud plopped out of her ear and landed in the crease of her book. Laura had her finger hooked around the white cord. The noise from the lunchroom chatter and the object falling in the line of her sight distracted her. Brynn hated being distracted when she was focused on something important, like making the grades she needed to get into the college of her dreams. She turned her eyes up to Laura who sat beside her, purple ponytail high on her head, black-lined, brown-eyed stare set on Cassidy and the pom-pom squad.

"Beware, she's headed this way," Laura said.

"Why do I need to beware?" Brynn mumbled as she stuck her earbud back in her left ear. The music was low enough she could still hear Laura without missing out on track five, which would totally go onto a playlist when Brynn got home and could sync her iPod. "She never stops at our table. We're *so* not on her radar."

"Don't sound so disappointed," Laura teased.

"Who said I was disappointed? I kinda like it." Brynn looked up and tilted her head, considering what would happen if Cassidy Rivers actually noticed her existence.

Hmm… probably nothing.

They both watched as Cassidy *I'm-destined-to-be-prom-queen* Rivers swished on by their table, her bleach-bottle-blonde besties flanking both sides. A few of the brain-dead jocks that always followed them around fell in behind the three girls. It was so tragically cliché and so *After School Special.*

Brynn couldn't stand it, or so she kept telling herself.

Keep on walking, girl. Keep on walking, she thought as Cassidy and her clique rounded the edge of the table. Brynn pulled in a deep breath, kept her head low, and only watched them through the part in her pink, chin-length, straight-as-a-freakin'-board hair. She reached up and tugged at one of the six silver loops hanging from either ear—a nervous habit she'd recently developed—and casually kept her black-lined eyes fixed on Cassidy.

A white cashmere sweater clung to Cassidy's slight curves and met at the pink skirt hugging her waist and thighs. The skirt stopped just above the knee, and below that was a pair of white, high-heeled boots that reached all the way up past her calves. The outfit had to be designer. It had that classy look to it. But what really caught Brynn's eye was the golden pendant hanging from Cassidy's neck. It looked Celtic—a knot of some sort—with lots of loops and weaves. Brynn had seen something like it before in one of her cool Gothic jewelry catalogs, but the one around Cassidy's neck didn't look like a cheap knockoff. It looked like the real deal—maybe priceless, maybe even antique. It definitely gave Miss Better-Than-Everyone-Else a depth she didn't have before.

Cassidy and crew kept walking but not without smirking down at Brynn like she was the scum of the earth. Something wicked flickered in that girl's big blue-gray eyes, something mean and totally deceiving to the rest of the world—the ones who believed Cassidy was as innocent as the Virgin Mary or something.

Pfft!

"Looks like we got lucky again," Laura whispered as soon as the in-crowd cleared the table.

Brynn finally exhaled, little strands of pink hair fluttering in the breeze. Yeah, they got lucky again, but they always got lucky. They were such an insignificant blip Cassidy didn't even bother, not like the poor nerd-herd the jocks loved to bully three tables back.

Something stupid and curious came over Brynn. For some dumb reason, she glanced over her shoulder to see what they were doing. The jocks were hovering over the nerds. Cassidy and the blonde squad worked their way over to the table where the cheerleaders and the other popular kids always sat, but for some messed-up reason, Cassidy kept watching her. If Brynn didn't turn around now and mind her own business, she knew she would be on the receiving end of some snarky comment, and honestly, Brynn would rather study calculus than get into a battle of wits with the unarmed.

"Why is she staring at us?" Laura asked.

"I don't know." Brynn turned back to her book. "Just don't look at her, and maybe she'll forget we exist."

"Yeah. Maybe."

"Hey, it's worked for two years, hasn't it? I mean like, we're seniors now, and we haven't been bullied by her or her friends. She doesn't even waste her time with us. So, let's just keep doing what we've been doing and pretend she doesn't exist either."

"Right," Laura said as she looked down at her lunch tray and the massive helping of beef surprise that had started out as meatloaf at the beginning of the week.

Jeez, Brynn didn't see how Laura could eat that crap. It smelled like something died on a plate, and the lovely Lunch Lady Brigade couldn't wait to serve that slop up to the unsuspecting masses. She cringed and began gathering up her books, then grabbed her backpack from the chair beside her. Brynn tucked her iPod into the pocket of her black hoodie and said to Laura, "See you in sixth period."

"Yeah. Totally. Good luck on the exam."

"Thanks," Brynn muttered before heading out of the cafeteria.

She wandered down the nearly empty hallway, past all the bright red lockers, platform boots thumping against the white linoleum. The bell hadn't rung yet, so most of the other students were still in their classes or hanging out in the cafeteria. Brynn liked the halls like that. She didn't have to push through the crowds, didn't have to fight her way through the cliquey circles just to get to her locker. She could take her time and just… chill.

Brynn hugged her black hoodie tight around her body as she headed up the stairwell to the second floor. The Donnas' latest album played from her iPod and spilled some of her favorite music into her ears. She'd made it all the way to track eleven, and it would probably end right before she made it to her class.

She thought about Cassidy, about how mean and snarky the girl could be. Brynn wondered if that was the real Cassidy or just a show she put on to be the popular girl, because being part of the in-crowd came with certain responsibilities—which apparently included walking all over everyone else in the school. Whatever. It wouldn't matter much longer. They had one semester left before they graduated. She would go off to college, and Cassidy would… do something with her empty, narcissistic life. Not that Brynn cared what Cassidy did after high school.

Or wait, did she?

Ugh!

The bell rang just as Brynn hit the second floor. Doors opened. Chatter filled the halls. People came barreling by as they went to their lockers. Brynn dropped her backpack off at hers. She tucked everything away in the cramped metal locker, then slammed the door and twisted the knob to lock it back into place. Just as she spun on her two-inch platform heels, she came face-to-face with the one person in the entire school she'd done a real good job of avoiding.

Cassidy Rivers.

"Why were you staring at me, freak?" Cassidy all but spat at Brynn—manicured brows arched, arms crossed over her chest, perfect pink nails tapping against her upper arms.

"I… um…," Brynn stuttered, hugging herself a little tighter.

"'I… um…' what? Did you see something you like?"

"Your necklace," Brynn blurted for God only knew what reason.

Cassidy laid her palm over the golden knot, but she didn't look away from Brynn, didn't look any less put off by Brynn's presence. Her pink lips pursed, but she didn't say a word. In fact, neither of them said anything. They just kept staring at each other because apparently, neither of them knew how to speak anymore.

"Well," Cassidy finally said, nostrils flaring, upper lip curling in disgust, "maybe you should find something else to ogle, because I don't appreciate being the object of your affection."

And with those last biting words, Cassidy pushed by Brynn with so much force it made her stumble to the side. Brynn swung back around, glaring at the back of Cassidy's body as she sauntered over toward her clique.

"You don't have to be so mean," Brynn yelled across the way. "I mean, I was going to tell you the necklace was neat… that's all, but really, it looks ridiculous on you."

Cassidy twirled around again. The kids surrounding her all laughed. She kicked out one booted foot and cocked her hip to the side, one hand resting at her waist while the other arm held her pink purse.

"Jealous, Nightmare On My Street?"

"What?" *What the hell did that mean?*

"Are. You. Jealous. Of. Me. Brynn?" she asked slowly, enunciating every word.

"No, as a matter of fact, I'm not. I pity you." *What a lie.*

"You"—Cassidy pointed to Brynn, then thumbed back at herself—"pity me? You *have* to be kidding. I have what everyone wants. What do you have?"

Well, as a matter of fact, Brynn had brains, and she was cute but not vain. She had the best friend anyone could ask for and two very loving parents. She had good grades and a ticket out of suburban

California. She had everything she wanted... except the one person she'd been most fascinated with her entire high school career.

Instead of some biting, snarky comeback, Brynn hugged her book tighter and looked away. She absolutely refused to play this game with Cassidy, especially in front of all Cassidy's friends. She would only be laughed at, and right now, she had more important things to worry about.

She pushed through the group of popular kids as they laughed and teased her. Despite their bullying, she didn't let them get to her. She ignored them as she continued down the hall to her calculus class, and she sat down at her desk as if none of that had ever happened. Brynn painted a smile on her face—as fake as it was—pulled out her pencil and her book, and readied herself for that stupid exam. Soon enough, the day would be over, and she could drown her miseries in a little music, maybe even a Tim Burton classic.

Yes, she really was *that* stereotypical.

Chapter 2

"UGH, the nerve of that spaz," Cassidy muttered under her breath, more to herself than to Jenna, one of her friends who'd caught up to her.

She hiked her pink Juicy Couture purse up onto her shoulder and stopped at the locker where she kept the textbooks for her second-floor classes. Some ugly, no-name, nerdy kid with a crush had offered his locker to her at the beginning of the year so she wouldn't have to carry her books up and down the stairs. Who was going to argue with that?

"What spaz?" Jenna asked, leaning one sun-kissed, bare shoulder against the locker beside Cassidy's. She had an inquisitive look in her eyes, the one she got right before she went all Judge Judy and started with her 977 questions.

Cassidy wasn't going to take the bait. Her lunch was still digesting. The apple and raspberry salad she'd brought from home would surely come up if she had to admit to speaking to that Frankenbride, Brynn. Gah, what had she been thinking? Why did she approach her like that? She would be the social outcast of the century if anyone saw her talking to the creepy emo girl from Loserville with that wannabe friend of hers, Laura or Laurie or something.

"What spaz?" Jenna pressed again.

This time, she tapped her French-manicured acrylic nails against the metal locker door as a show of impatience. *Really? Who did she think she was?* Cassidy Rivers didn't answer to anyone until she was good and ready, and she wasn't anywhere near good or ready to talk about Brynn.

"Some loser who bumped into me. Forget it," she replied in a tone that told Jenna to call off her inquisition.

It worked. Jenna pushed off the locker and shrugged her shoulders in indifference, causing the spaghetti straps of her tank top to slide down. She was impossibly thin and bony, and sometimes Cassidy swore the chick took the finger-to-the-throat approach after eating. Whenever she did eat, that was.

"Whatevs. I'm gonna head to Government and Economics. See you at practice after school." It wasn't even a question.

Cassidy almost replied with her systematic "yeah."

She had been on the cheerleading squad since her freshman year and never missed a single practice. She was the captain of the squad and had a regional cheer competition to train for, but her mom had pleaded with her to come straight home after school because her grandmother, aka Nana, was coming into town for a while, and they were supposed to pick her up from the airport.

She'd complained and argued, dramatically pointing out that it was going to ruin her life if she lost regionals because her mother was too codependent to make a simple airport run. In the end, however, her mom gave her the sad look she reserved for guilt trips, which were usually followed by the "I'm doing the best I can as a single mother" speech, and Cassidy agreed. Reluctantly and tight-browed, but she'd agreed nonetheless.

"I won't be at practice today," Cassidy replied curtly. "Gotta go do this thing with my mom. Lead the squad in the basic formations and get them tighter on their finishing routine."

Jenna's toffee-colored eyes grew so wide Cassidy feared they would pop out of their sockets, and the eyeball juice would ruin her Michael Kors cashmere sweater.

Before her friend started in on another round of questions, Cassidy shut her locker door and turned to walk away, leaving Jenna still standing there, mouth agape. Whatever. She was cocaptain. She could deal.

As if she was going to admit to picking up her grandmother. *Puh-leeeease.* Who in the world skipped cheer practice to hang out with old people? Well, secretly, she did, but it wasn't anyone's business. As a matter of fact, as she walked down the hall to her fifth-period biology class, she reiterated to herself for the thousandth time that day, none of the people she called her friends really knew much at all about the real her.

She worked hard to maintain her image. Cassidy Rivers was the popular girl. She was the captain of the varsity cheerleading squad, senior class president, and the one with the expensive clothes and brand new car. She only had the coolest friends and was always the determining voice in what, or who, was in or out. She ran the school fundraisers and headed the pep rally coordination, as well as governed over the homecoming dance preparation. She was the girl every other girl wanted to be.

And yet, she wasn't herself at all.

She walked into the classroom, took her usual seat in the back row of desks, and stared out the large bay window to her left. The bright California sunshine beckoned her, just as nature always did. She always felt compelled to go outside and enjoy the breeze, bask in the warmth of the sun, or appreciate the beauty of the beaches. The trees seemed to whisper her name, dropping leaves in a show of respect as she walked by. When lit, candles flickered a little brighter around her. Water changed to perfect temperature without her having to adjust the knobs. Even the air around her crackled with energy. Energy people thought came from her attitude, but in reality was just her magic.

Yes, the real Cassidy Rivers came from a long line of witches dating back almost two hundred years before the Salem trials. No pointy shoes, though. Ugh. As if. Like the devil, witches wore Prada too. She looked down at her heeled boots to silently affirm that statement.

That Witch!

So she was a witch, but of course, no one knew. Actually, she didn't want the magic that bugged the heck out of her more and more each day. As a younger girl, it was nothing more than an odd attraction to all things in nature, but as she grew, so did the darn powers. If she wasn't careful, she could expose herself with something as absentminded as snapping her fingers—which had recently proven to light *all* the candles in her bedroom one evening, scaring the crap out of her cat, Louie, in the process.

She only had the cat because the darn thing had followed her home when he was a kitten and refused to leave. She let him sit outside for three days before finally asking her mom if he could come inside. Her mother agreed all too quickly, which was weird for a woman who didn't even approve of pet fish, but whatever.

"Good afternoon, class. Please open your textbooks to page eighty-two and silently read the lesson on cellular respiration." Mrs. Wright's gritty voice broke her away from her thoughts. She grabbed the book sitting on her desk and flipped the hard cover open, ready to turn to the chapter she needed to read. But when she looked down, the name scribbled across the inside made her huff in exasperation. "Brynn Michaels."

Ugh, what was it with that chick already? And why was she eyeballing her necklace earlier? The same necklace Nana had given her when she turned thirteen, along with a ridiculously long speech about the responsibilities tied to their heritage, the powers she would be coming into, yada yada yada. Truth be told, she wasn't really listening then, and she refused to pay any more attention to Brynn today too.

Chapter 3

"TIME'S up," Mrs. Temple said from behind her desk. Pencils clacked against wooden desktops. Students sat back in their chairs. Some had confident smiles on their faces. Others looked scared to death. Brynn felt good about this exam. There weren't too many equations that had tripped her up. That last minute studying she'd done during lunch really helped, despite the pause for the Cassidy Rivers show.

"Pass your papers forward."

Mrs. Temple stood from her chair and walked down the front of each row of desks, peasant skirt elegantly flowing behind her as she strode across the room to collect the finished tests. Her light-brown hair was pulled back in a tight bun as always, brown-eyed stare looking over the class, sizing up each and every student, even though she probably already knew who'd passed and who'd failed.

The bell rang, and most of Brynn's fellow classmates scattered like rats from a burning building. Brynn hung back to avoid the crowded rush and the lackadaisical bodies meandering through the halls. She quietly gathered her book and pen and the notebook that went everywhere with her. It was filled with all her silly, random musings—from things she loved to things that bothered her, and little notes about songs and bands or books she wanted to remember. The equivalent of a journal, she supposed.

Brynn made her way out to the crowded hall, pushing past all the tragically hip and the devastatingly beautiful, through the nerds huddling around their comic books and the jocks who hit on cheerleaders every chance they got. She navigated through the masses and back toward her locker to grab the book for her next class.

Lost in thought, she dug through her locker, oblivious to anything and everything around her. She kept her face hidden, just in case Cassidy wanted to taunt her again. She thought if she could just avoid any more confrontation today, everything would be okay, and she could go back to being another invisible blip far off Cassidy Rivers's radar. She kept her head low until her bestie, Laura, popped up beside her.

"So, how did it go?" Laura asked, plum lips spread in a smile as she tucked her purple-dyed hair behind her multipierced ear.

"Good, I guess," Brynn quietly responded as she slung her backpack over her shoulder. She had everything ready to go, all the books she needed for her homework, so when the last bell of the day rang, she could bolt straight out to her car without having to fight through the circles of all the other students. "There wasn't anything I couldn't answer."

"Awesomeness!"

"Yeah." Brynn laughed softly. "You coming over tonight for movies and pizza?"

"Well, duh! It's Friday night, right?"

"True story. Mom wants to take me shopping tomorrow, but I totally don't want to go."

As soon as Brynn turned from her locker, she spotted Cassidy charging her way through the crowd like a rabid beast. Okay, maybe that was a huge exaggeration. Maybe Cassidy was sauntering or taking light, even steps. But every time Brynn saw Miss Perfect Princess, her mind conjured images of evil witches with hooked noses and monsters from the great beyond. Though truthfully, Cassidy didn't resemble any of those things. She was beautiful, too beautiful, and maybe that's why Brynn painted a horrific picture of the girl most likely to become a supermodel.

"What are you looking at?" Cassidy snapped, but she didn't stop walking. She didn't wait for Brynn's response.

Brynn would've lied anyway. She would've said she'd been checking out that crazy knotted necklace hanging from Cassidy's neck, but truth be told, it was Cassidy she couldn't take her eyes off of. As much as she hated Cassidy Rivers as a person, she couldn't help the bizarre attraction she had to the other girl.

"Earth to Brynn," Laura said, waving her hand in front of Brynn's face. "You in there?"

Brynn shook her head. "Huh? What? Yeah, I'm here."

"God, why would you stare at her like that? Don't you know better by now?"

"I don't know what came over me."

"Whatever it was, you'd better get over it fast before you end up as a big red dot on Cassidy's radar."

True story. Very, very true. When Cassidy locked in on a target, she didn't forget them until they were completely and utterly destroyed, and Brynn didn't want to be a last-minute name added to Cassidy's "pulverize before high school is over" list.

"Can we just go?" Brynn said as she took her first steps away from her locker. Laura promptly followed, hanging tight to Brynn's back.

Keeping her head down like always, Brynn made her way through the ambling students and hallway loiterers, down to the last door on the left. Her sixth-period teacher—a tiny, frail woman with gnarled fingers, a bright white granny hairdo, and wire-rimmed bifocals on the tip of her nose—stood at the end of the hallway, yelling at boisterous students about getting to class. No one listened to her. They didn't show her an ounce of respect. She was sweet, and they were horrible for treating her the way they did. No one would ever do anything about it and the woman wouldn't take up for herself, and unfortunately, she probably should've retired years ago.

"Hi, Mrs. Miller," Brynn said in passing as she entered her last class of the day.

"Hello, Miss Michaels."

Brynn gave her a soft smile, then headed over to the desk she'd chosen at the beginning of the school year. It was right up front so she could hear Mrs. Miller read from classic American novels over the low chatter of students who just didn't seem to care. Choosing that spot had garnered her all sorts of petty nicknames—from brownnoser to teacher's pet. Not that Brynn cared enough to pay attention. Some stuff simply didn't matter in the grand scheme of things.

She sat down, Laura taking her normal spot right beside her, and leaned over into her bag to pull out her textbook, when she caught the scent of flowers wafting by her. It was Cassidy's perfume. Brynn would never forget that scent as long as she lived. It smelled of roses and jasmine, with a hint of vanilla to soften the overall ambrosia. The smell of it brought a dreamy-eyed smile to Brynn's face.

"What are you grinning about?" Laura whispered, leaning in close so no one else would hear her.

"I uh... um...."

"Tell me you weren't smiling at Cassidy. She's toxic."

Intoxicating, maybe. "God, no! Why would I smile at her? She's totally vapid."

"True, but...." Laura glanced over her shoulder at Cassidy, then back to Brynn, as if *that* wasn't obvious. Might as well hang a "we're talking about you" sign around both their necks. "You've been watching her a lot lately. Is there something I need to know about?"

"No!" Brynn blurted.

No, there wasn't anything anyone needed to know. As far as anyone else was concerned, Brynn and Cassidy were and always would be mortal enemies.

"Don't bite my head off, sheesh!"

"I'm not. I just...." Brynn shook her head.

She closed her trap and righted herself in her seat the moment she heard the classroom door slam and their dainty English teacher begin to speak. Mrs. Miller called the room to attention and took attendance. That ate away about three minutes of class.

Brynn stayed in her own happy, little bubble, counting away the minutes until Mrs. Miller graced them with a quick read. She daydreamed of lying on her bed, reading or listening to music—maybe some Anne Rice and a little Secondhand Serenade. God, that sounded so incredible right now. Her Zen.

"I have a project for you," Mrs. Miller said, and immediately Brynn snapped to attention. "We're going to do a literary scavenger hunt. Five books, one for every month, then a report at the end of the school year. It will be half of your final grade."

Well, Brynn had no problem with that. American literature was her strongest subject. She knew authors and poets and loved it all. This assignment would give her a perfect grade and kick her GPA up into Ivy League level.

"This is going to be a group project," Mrs. Miller continued. It still wasn't a problem. Brynn could work with Laura and everything would be great because they worked so well together. Then the dainty old English teacher said, "I'm assigning partners."

Brynn bit down on her bottom lip to keep from cursing.

"Laura, I want you paired up with Sarah."

Wait. No. What? Laura is my *partner!*

She gave her best friend a *this-can't-be-happening* look as their teacher called out the remaining groups. Brynn couldn't imagine not working with Laura. This had to be a mistake.

"Brynn Michaels and Cassidy Rivers," Mrs. Miller said.

And Brynn's worst nightmare came true.

"No!" both girls said in perfect unison as they bolted up from their respective desks. Brynn's stare shot to the back corner of the classroom. Cassidy's glare pierced right through her. This would never,

ever work. She couldn't talk to Cassidy, let alone work on a school project with the bubbly cheerleader.

Failure was imminent.

There went Brynn's perfect GPA.

There went her Ivy League dreams.

Chapter 4

CASSIDY stood at the very back of the class, arms crossed beneath her small breasts as she glared daggers at Mrs. Miller. "You can't be serious!" she protested. "I won't work with Marie Laveau. She smells like dusty voodoo dolls and cat carcasses!"

The old lady didn't seem to care. Her ice-blue gaze shifted slowly to Brynn. She offered the weirdo a sympathetic half smile before refocusing on Cassidy.

"Miss Rivers, it is impolite to call your peers names. If you don't want to do the assignment, you can fail my class," she said, with all the calm in the world.

"But, Mrs. Miller!"

"No buts. The partner assignments are final. Now, please sit down so I may continue."

"Mrs. Miller, she's crazy! I can't work with her!"

The moment she spat out those words, something rippled beneath her skin. She felt the fizzing and buzzing of electric energy in her hands. *No. Not now. Please not now.* She tried not to panic as she balled her fingers into fists at her side.

"Miss Rivers, you will sit down and be quiet or you'll go to the principal's office," Mrs. Miller warned. This time, the lady's voice held a solid tone of resolve and authority that matched the final stare she shot at Cassidy. She held her gaze steady, as if daring her to utter another syllable.

Glaring harder, Cassidy stomped her designer boot-clad foot down against the linoleum floor, creating a thump that echoed across the silent classroom. The fizzling held strong, even as Cassidy took slow breaths. The other students stared in either awe or sympathy. All eyes were on her except for Brynn's. The freak sat ducked so low into her seat, if she sank down one more inch, her face would hit the edge of the desk.

"This sucks!" Cassidy mumbled.

Huffing, she threw herself back into her seat, ignoring the kids who were still staring at her as if she were a petulant child throwing a temper tantrum. She didn't care. Nothing mattered at the moment except the certainty of her soon-to-be catastrophic social homicide and that familiar, unwanted churn of witchy energy coursing through her body.

Her mind raced with images of her friends laughing behind her back, whispering that she had to miss cheer practice just to work with the Bride of Frankenstein. The boys would stop fawning over her— something that didn't really bother her since she never paid attention to them anyways, but they made life easier by offering to carry her books and wash her car. Plus, the jocks always followed her around like puppies waiting for a bone, willing to do anything it took to get her attention. That would all come to a screeching halt the moment she was forced to interact with Freakzilla in public.

Or not....

Maybe, just maybe, if she could only deal with Brynn outside of school, Cassidy could get away with finishing this stupid project without becoming a total outcast. It was the only hope she had of surviving the potential assassination of her social status. And now that she'd figured out a way to save herself, the fizzling started to subside, and Cassidy felt like she could actually relax again.

When she glanced up from the closed English book on her desk, she saw Brynn peering back at her through the crease in her bangs. The moment Brynn caught her looking, the freak whipped around and sank lower—if that was even possible—into her chair. Cassidy only admitted to herself that the girl's tresses were a pretty shade of pink.

Brynn's hair was pale and reminded her of cotton candy. As far as Cassidy remembered, Brynn had naturally tawny hair, but sometime over the summer, she'd changed it to the shade it was now. It suited her. The color complimented her usual black clothing and added a hint of femininity to her otherwise hard-rock edge. It made her slightly more approachable.

The truth was, Brynn Michaels scared the hell out of Cassidy. The way she walked around not caring about what people thought about her indicated that she was either entirely too confident or she had the emotional vacuity of a serial killer. She didn't have any friends save for the reject sitting beside her, nor did she ever seem interested in making any. She never involved herself with school events or functions, and she shied away from anything involving sports. What could she be doing with all her spare time? She could be skinning animals and performing satanic rituals after school—a thought that made Cassidy shudder.

As Mrs. Miller continued to rattle off partner assignments, several kids in the class mumbled unhappily while others squealed softly, no doubt because they'd been paired with someone they liked. Her friend Michelle had just gotten stuck with one of the leaders of the nerd-herd, Ryan Daniels. The kid was one pocket protector away from fulfilling the textbook definition of geekdom. He was a mathlete, the president of the Physics club, on the Chess team, and a junior member of one of the research groups that had recently discovered the Higgs boson particle. He had braces, glasses, and perfectly combed-over hair, which he used entirely too much gel on. The clothes he wore were straight out of a J. Crew catalog, complete with penny loafer shoes.

Cassidy would take all that nerdiness over Brynn's freakiness any day.

When the teacher who had ruined her life in a matter of seconds finished playing social cupid, she began to read a chapter aloud to the class. Her voice fell back to a soft, almost inaudible pitch. Funny how the old bat could talk loudly enough to put her in her place but she couldn't stay loud so everyone could actually hear what the hell she was reading. Cassidy flipped through the pages in her book, trying to find where Mrs. Miller was reading from. The boy next to her, Zach, leaned over and whispered, "Page 268."

"Thanks," she muttered back. He looked surprised that she'd thanked him. Gawd, she *was* capable of being nice... sometimes.

She found the chapter and tried to follow along, but Mrs. Miller's voice whispered so low she only caught a word every other sentence, so she just speed-read through the whole thing and finished early. With that done, she moved along and answered the questions on the quiz at the end of the chapter, taking her time to go back and search for an answer when she wasn't quite sure. The whole time she worked, Mrs. Miller droned on in the distance, voice fading more and more with every sentence read.

Cassidy swore her hatred for the old battle-axe grew as her voice dimmed. By the time the teacher finished reading, Cassidy was all but snarling at her from her seat in the back of the class, where the cool kids always sat, purposely to avoid having to hear the old coot.

"Please use the time remaining to complete the quiz following the chapter and bring your papers up to my desk once you're finished," Mrs. Miller instructed before she cracked open a water bottle and took a sip in what was probably an effort to dislodge the spiderwebs in her old throat.

Cassidy tore along the perforated edge of the page, removing it from the textbook. The moment she rose from her seat, proud of herself for having had the foresight to finish before everyone else, Brynn also stood.

Un-freaking-believable!

They hadn't been paired together an hour and already the spaz was trying to outshine her. Pfft. She had another thing coming. Cassidy sped up to the front of the class, darting past Brynn and damn near shoving her out of the way.

"Hey!" Freakzilla called out softly, righting herself.

Cassidy ignored her.

With a cocky smile, Cassidy set her paper down on a desk that looked as old and faded as the teacher. "I finished first," she pointed out, rather pretentiously. Mrs. Miller only nodded, resembling a shaky baby vulture who couldn't quite hold up the weight of its head.

When Brynn stood on the opposite side of the desk and placed her paper in the box labeled *Completed Work*, Mrs. Miller smiled proudly at her, offering her a gently spoken, "Very good, Miss Michaels."

What. The. Heck. Everrrrrr.

Cassidy rolled her eyes and huffed exaggeratedly before turning on her heels and flipping her blonde hair over her shoulder in an I-don't-care move. When she got back to her desk, she began packing her stuff up. Something inside her—deep, *deep* down inside—tingled when she thought of the moment she'd pushed Brynn aside. Their hips had brushed together for a split second, and in retrospect, she could admit to wanting to feel more of Brynn's pliant body against her.

Before she could stop herself from daydreaming, her libido trampled her logic. In a flash, she fantasized about what Brynn looked like beneath all those black clothes. Images of her flawless, pale skin flashed through her mind, bared naked for her eyes. Brynn's pouty lips parted, and her eyes fluttered closed in ecstasy over what Cassidy's mouth did to her in her mind's eye.

Cassidy clenched her legs together beneath the desk, and a bright blush crept up on her cheeks. She ducked her head down, allowing her hair to cover her face. As if being a witch wasn't bad enough, Cassidy was also into girls. She repressed that little secret even more than she did her magic, because come on, her friends would freak out if they had to shower and change in the same locker room with someone who could secretly be checking out their boobs. Not that she saw any of her friends in that light, but they wouldn't be smart enough to figure it out or listen to reason.

When the bell rang, she stormed toward the front of the class once more, pushing past Brynn. A few kids snickered. Brynn didn't protest, and Cassidy kept trying to dislodge the naughty visions from her head. *Great.* This was what she would have to work with for the next five months, as well as deal with the possible repercussions of being seen with Brynn in public.

Yeah, life just went from good to mortifying.

Chapter 5

EVERY single student, save for Brynn and Laura, bolted out of the classroom. They had a new eagerness to get out the door. After all, the shrill sound of the bell echoing down the hall meant the end of the school day, and even better, the start of the weekend.

Mrs. Miller followed her students out into the hallway to pull her never-ending crowd control duty. Brynn stood rigid, still totally freaking over her brush with Evil in Pink. Of course, in Cassidy's mind, Brynn had obviously been in *her* way. After all, Cassidy ruled the school, and that land was her land… no one else's. She made the law, and she could do no wrong.

"And I'm stuck working with her for the rest of the year…," Brynn mumbled.

"I totally can't believe Mrs. Miller paired you two. Is she blind or something? Does she live under a rock? Everyone knows you and Cassidy don't get along."

"Cassidy and I don't speak to each other," Brynn said flatly, giving Laura a droll expression. "Our rivalry isn't catastrophic enough to register on the Richter scale."

"True." Laura shrugged. "But still. Popular people with popular people. Everyone knows that."

"Maybe." Brynn hiked her backpack up on her shoulder. "I'm gonna go. See you tonight?"

"Yeah. I'm bringing movies."

"'K, see you then."

Laura eagerly snatched up her backpack and headed out the door. Brynn promptly followed, slowing into an aimless amble as she wove through the mass of bodies rushing through the halls to get their Friday nights started. Her platform boots thumped against the linoleum. Her stare stayed trained on the floor, but somehow she managed to move through the crowd without any embarrassing accidents.

Through the small group of not-so-eager loiterers, Brynn spotted the bright red door leading into the girls' bathroom. She took the long route, avoiding the crowd as best as she could, then pressed her palm to the door. Its hinges creaked as it opened, and the moment she ducked inside, she saw Cassidy Rivers, fixing her already perfect pink lipstick in the mirror.

Brynn froze.

Cassidy looked up.

Brynn swore World War III was about to erupt in the only girls' bathroom on that floor.

She wasn't going to say a word. Brynn intended on going straight down to the stall, taking care of business, then hauling out of there before a riot ensued. But when she saw Cassidy's smirking reflection and wicked blue eyes watching her, something inside her snapped. She'd had enough.

"Cassidy—"

"What?" Cassidy barked at her.

"Why do you hate me so much? What did I ever do to you?"

"You're a freak. That's all there is to it."

"So," Brynn said, crossing her arms over her chest and shifting from one heel to the other. "You mean to tell me that because I don't wear bright colors and don't like Katy Perry or hanging out at the mall that I'm not worthy of a little respect. Are you really that shallow?"

"Shallow? Hold up. First of all, I don't give a rat's furry ass what you're into or not into. You have, like, zero friends. You're always alone. You don't care for group activities. In other words, you're like a serial killer in training."

"I have friends! I spend my time studying. I have a 4.0 GPA, thank you. I volunteer too. How does that make me a serial killer?"

"You have *one* friend. That hardly constitutes as a group of friends. Besides, I don't have to explain myself to you or anyone. What do you care if I like you or not?"

"Because, unfortunately, we have to work together for this stupid class." Brynn exhaled sharply, looked down at her boots, then over to Cassidy's designer heels. She knew she would never be anything more than a weirdo in Cassidy's eyes, and this whole argument was one big waste of time, but she had to get her feelings off her chest, even if it did make her seem completely hopeless. "You could give me a chance," she muttered beneath her breath.

"A chance? No thanks, I'm fresh out of extra blood to donate to your satanic rituals. Just because we have to work together doesn't mean we have to like each other. Stay out of my way, and I'll stay out of yours. Somehow, we have to find time for this project, but I'll be damned if I'm seen hanging out with you, so figure it out."

"Fine. Whatever."

Brynn tucked tail and turned for the door, but the moment she reached for the handle, something stopped her, something stupid and hopeful, something she would probably regret saying in the end. She looked over her shoulder and said, "And all this time I thought—no, I hoped—there was more to you than this. Guess I was wrong."

"If you only knew…," Cassidy whispered, but the door had already closed, and Brynn Michaels was long gone.

Something inside her stung. Like her heart was having trouble dealing with the severity of the words she'd just sharply spat at Brynn.

In truth, she hadn't intended on being so mean to the girl. When she first walked into the bathroom, Cassidy almost smiled at her. After all, she had just been fantasizing about doing not-so-Catholic things to the girl just moments before. Then something made her go all feral, though, just like she always did. Even when Brynn hadn't done or said anything to deserve it, she immediately slammed her wall down and raised her defenses.

It annoyed her that she acted the way she did, but she didn't know how else to be. She'd been this person for so very long it became her default. What would Brynn have done if Cassidy had smiled and offered to work side by side with her on the project instead? She probably would've bolted from the bathroom, screaming about possession. And *Brynn* was supposed to be the satanist. Ha. Yeah, right.

Her lip gloss container clicked against the rest of the makeup in the small clutch holding the few essentials she carried around. While some considered her plastic, she wore very little makeup—some mascara, a little lip gloss, and a bit of blush to accent her sun-kissed cheeks. That was all she ever really needed.

She finished packing up her stuff and turned to head out the door, resolved to try and be a little bit nicer to Brynn. Okay, maybe not "nicer." Not right away. But perhaps she could start to be… civil?

There was just something about Brynn that had gotten under her skin. Something that—for some reason—chipped away at the guards she held up so tightly.

She didn't really notice there was a bit of a hurry to her step as she made her way out of the bathroom and down the hallway. Knowing where Brynn's locker was, she refused to acknowledge the little spark that ignited when she saw Brynn standing there, pink head hidden behind the red metal door. When she approached her, it wasn't the way she'd always done before. There was no hostility, no inner anger. She slowed down, suddenly unsure of what to say.

"Um," Cassidy stammered, "so listen. What if we work together on this one thing, and when it's over, we go back to not knowing each other, 'kay?"

"Yeah. Sure." Brynn frowned, tucking a pink tendril of fallen hair behind her ear. "But why—"

"Because we need the grade."

"Right. The grade. So, um... where do you wanna work or... whatever?"

"You know which house is mine. We live in the same neighborhood, so just come by my place," Cassidy said, as she fished in her bag for something to write with. She took Brynn's hand and scribbled her cell phone number across the pulse point of her wrist in pink glitter ink. "Guys would kill for that number. Don't give it out, 'kay?"

"No. Yeah. Right," Brynn stuttered, curling her hand and staring down at her wrist. Cassidy could feel the muscle in Brynn's arm flex against her palm and she immediately let go. "So, I'll, um... call you tomorrow?"

"Yeah, tomorrow works. Any time after noon."

"Sure. Thanks for...."

Brynn's words trailed off, and Cassidy was dying to know what she wanted to say next, but she didn't push. Instead, she nodded and muttered, "You're welcome," before turning around and heading back down the hallway and to the staircase.

Chapter 6

THE entire drive home, Brynn thought about how Cassidy had come back to her locker, how her whole demeanor had changed, about the way Cassidy's hand had felt around hers. The gentleness of her touch and the way her skin felt so soft did something to Brynn. It gave her a goofy grin and a warm feeling that radiated out from her chest and sent tingles down her arms. Cassidy actually made her smile for the first time in like… ever.

At least Cassidy didn't act like she hated her. At least right now, anyway.

Brynn pulled into the suburbs, past all the cookie-cutter look-alikes, past Cassidy Rivers's house, around the corner, and down to her own driveway. One block separated their houses. One block. But so much more kept them apart. Her house looked exactly like Cassidy's, save for the gardens, the arrangement of the flowers, and the fixtures. Brynn's house had an American flag flapping by the front door—a show of support since her daddy was a retired Air Force captain. Other than that, the houses were the same shape and color, had the same windows and doors. The same. But they were two very, very different girls.

She parked in her driveway, turned the car off, and grabbed her backpack from the passenger seat. As she worked her way toward the front door, she stole another quick glance at her wrist—the place where Cassidy had so gently and flawlessly written her phone number in pink

ink and huge, swooshing, bubbly strokes. The sight of it made Brynn smile. Though why she liked seeing it there, she had no idea. Maybe she just liked the idea that Cassidy Rivers could be nice to her, like Miss Popularity didn't completely hate her.

Just as Brynn reached for the doorknob, she heard Laura's car whipping around the corner. The music hit her ears right before she saw Laura's black Honda barreling up the driveway. Brynn's mom hated when Laura did that, and she'd asked Laura not to more than once. Laura didn't listen well.

Brynn waited for her, watching as Laura popped out from the driver's-side door. Laura got to her house so fast Brynn wondered if she'd even bothered going home. Laura held up her arm, waving a stack of DVDs in her hand as she jogged up the concrete path to meet Brynn.

"You just getting home?" Laura asked.

"Yeah," Brynn said as she slipped the key in the doorknob.

"What took you so long to get here?"

"I got hung up at school." *Not a lie, but not the whole story either.*

"What happened?"

God, could she be any nosier? "I, um… stuff at my locker."

"Oh," Laura said.

When Brynn turned the key in the lock, her arm turned as well, exposing the phone number written on her wrist. She'd stopped thinking about it until Laura grabbed her arm and pulled it up to see the pink evidence of exactly what had kept Brynn at her locker after school.

Laura frowned. "Whose number is that?"

"It's…. Well…. I…."

"Brynn."

"It's Cassidy Rivers's number," Brynn blurted. Heat rushed her cheeks.

That Witch!

Laura's eyes widened as she released Brynn's arm. She stared, mouth agape, eyes still as big as saucers, but she didn't say a word. Not that she had to. The astonishment on her face was enough to make Brynn a little squirmy.

Looking away, Brynn opened the door to her house. Cool air rushed out and blasted against her blazing hot face. Relief. Sorta. Now she just needed Laura to quit staring at her like she'd lost her mind.

They headed inside—Laura going straight up to Brynn's room, Brynn going to the kitchen for sodas and popcorn. At least their normal routine would put some distance between the girls and give Brynn time to think about how she would explain Cassidy's number while Laura marinated in whatever ideas she conjured about Brynn and Cassidy's new relationship.

Relationship? What a weird word to use when considering the most popular girl in the school.

Shaking her head, Brynn reached in the cabinet and grabbed a bag of popcorn. She started it popping and listened closely as the kernels exploded in the bag. Even as she focused her attention on the red and white bag rotating inside the microwave, she couldn't stop thinking about Cassidy.

There was definitely an attraction there, one Brynn couldn't deny, but wouldn't admit to anyone else. It was a different kind of attraction, one she hadn't felt with anyone else before. She wanted to spend time with Cassidy, wanted to snuggle under the covers and feel Cassidy's arms around her. She wanted to feel Cassidy's mouth against hers, if nothing more than to know what her lip gloss tasted like. Brynn wondered if they could ever be friends on any kind of level or if she was too much of a pariah for Cassidy to ever be seen with. It was so silly, and Brynn didn't even know why she cared.

Okay, so that was a lie. She did know why she cared. A part of her wanted to have a place in Cassidy's world. Take away all the self-righteous, narcissistic, catty, vapid airheads and that left… well, not much of anything. No wonder Brynn stuck to her one and only friend.

Cassidy had to be different, though. There had to be more to her than the role she played for the popular masses. Right? She had depth, something Brynn would've never even considered before Cassidy came over to her locker. She'd seen something in the cheerleader's eyes, something almost caring and understanding, something that actually did wish for more than what she had. Or maybe Brynn was just wishing on a star.

The microwave dinged and ripped Brynn right away from her Cassidy fantasies. She popped open the door and grabbed the bag by its corner, then grabbed a bowl from the cabinet. On her way out, she stopped by the fridge and collected two sodas, then hightailed it upstairs to her bedroom.

She found Laura sitting on the edge of her bed, toying with the remote to the DVD player. "So what did you pick out for us?" Brynn asked as she sat one of the bottles of soda on the nightstand next to Laura.

"*Sweeney Todd*. The Tim Burton version."

"Awesome," Brynn said as she plopped down on the purple beanbag on the floor. "Are you still spending the night?"

"I guess," Laura muttered.

Clearly something was bothering her, but Laura had always been the type who wouldn't volunteer to talk about things unless someone else did the prying. Honestly, though, Brynn wasn't in the mood to pry. She had her own issues right now, issues she wouldn't share with anyone, and holding Laura's hand while she sulked wasn't a top priority.

The movie started to play as Brynn dumped half the popcorn into a bowl for Laura. Neither one of them said a word, even though they always talked through the movies they'd seen a hundred times or more. They'd seen *Sweeney Todd* a hundred and two times easy, even knew most of the words by heart. Yet Laura focused so hard on the television, she acted like she'd never seen the movie before.

"Okay, what's wrong with you?" Brynn asked, sitting forward on the beanbag.

"Why do you have Cassidy Rivers's number scribbled on your wrist?" Laura blurted as if the question had been playing on infinite loop in her brain. She didn't look at Brynn when she asked. Instead, she kept her wide eyes glued to the TV screen.

"We're working on a project together, remember?"

"Yeah," Laura muttered, but Brynn could tell she wasn't buying it.

"What? It's the truth. You were there when Mrs. Miller paired us together."

"Yeah, I was. But I also saw how mortified you both were when she said it. Cassidy clearly wasn't into the idea of doing anything with you."

"Maybe not, but we both have to make a good grade on this. Despite how Cassidy acts, she's always been a good student."

Laura's thick black brows arched as she swung her head in Brynn's direction. Her nostrils flared, and her lips curled. She stared at Brynn like she'd sprouted a third eye in the middle of her forehead.

"You're complimenting her now?" Laura all but yelped. The disbelief in her voice was almost as piercing as her glare.

"I wouldn't call that a compliment. It's just the truth."

"Are you gonna start taking up for her too?"

"No."

"You sure?"

"Yes."

Laura rolled her eyes, then turned her jet-black gaze back to the TV.

Sighing, Brynn settled back into her beanbag and tossed bits of popcorn into her mouth. She was glad the conversation was over but had the distinct feeling it hadn't ended. The topic of Cassidy Rivers and the pink phone number on Brynn's wrist would come up again. She could feel it almost as much as she could still feel the warmth of Cassidy's palm against the skin of her arm.

Chapter 7

WHEN Brynn woke up the next morning, her cheek was stuck to the vinyl surface of her giant purple beanbag. Her knees were curled into her chest, and a half-eaten bag of popcorn had spilled out on the gray carpet lining her bedroom. Laura nestled in Brynn's bed, sleeping like a baby. The menu to the last movie they'd watched filled the TV screen, music playing in a loop.

She looked down at her wrist, and thankfully, Cassidy's number was still there, though a little blurred. Brynn could barely make out the numbers, but she knew the moment the hot water of her morning shower hit her skin, the pink ink would completely vanish. Brynn couldn't have that. No way could she lose that number.

The room was still pretty dark, save for the flickering images from the TV and the hints of light peeking in from beneath the dark purple curtains hanging over the only window in Brynn's bedroom. She extracted herself from the beanbag, clumsily pushed up to her feet, and stumbled over to her desk, trying not to make too much noise so she wouldn't wake Laura.

Quietly, she clicked on the small lamp bent over her laptop. It didn't put off too much brightness, only enough to light the keys of her computer. It worked fine. She only needed to see enough to jot down Cassidy's phone number before the digits wore away.

Half awake, she blindly searched her desk for something to write with, fingers fumbling with the chaos of everything her mother had asked her more than once to straighten up. She had the coolest Gothic Tinker Bell stationery set her little sister had bought her for Christmas a few years back, and Brynn hadn't used it too often. The paper was just too pretty to waste on stupid scribblings.

Cassidy's phone number wasn't just some stupid scribbling, though.

She rolled her wrist over and jotted the digits down across one of Tinker Bell's wings, leaving off the name so nosy somebodies wouldn't know who the number belonged to. That little slip of paper was comparable to the most valuable treasure under the stars for some silly reason. It was her golden ticket to the chocolate factory. Even if hanging out with Cassidy Rivers didn't automatically make her one of the cool kids, at least she would get a little taste of life in the cheerleader's world.

After pinning the page to her black and purple memory board, Brynn grabbed a change of clothes from her closet and headed down the hallway to the bathroom. She'd picked out something cute to wear, something that would make her look less "homicidal" and more... normal, she guessed. It was an adorable dress and vest combo—white blouse, black skirt, black tie and vest. She even had the knee-high white socks and black patent Mary Janes to finish the look off.

Now, why she put so much importance into looking cute for Cassidy, she really didn't know. A mere twenty-four hours ago she wouldn't have cared. But apparently, twenty-four hours was enough time to make a whole lot of changes. In the span of one short day, Cassidy went from traumatizing and mortifying to almost sincere, and Brynn went from careful avoidance to absolutely dying to be closer to the queen of the school. And none of it made any sense.

Brynn climbed into the shower, stood beneath the hot jets of water, and let it rain down over her tightened muscles. Sleeping on the beanbag had knotted her neck, and only when the muscles finally started to loosen did she realize how painful it felt. She turned around and let the water pound against her knotted shoulders as she reached for her jasmine-scented bodywash.

Would Cassidy like that scent?

Would she consider it normal?

The thought made Brynn's eyes widen, made her stop brushing her purple, spongy pouf over her body. Her fingers tightened around the netted ball as she stared at the creme-colored shower tiles. If Brynn didn't get her head on straight, there was no way she would be able to face Cassidy today without making a complete fool of herself.

A knock at the door pulled her away from her silent mental breakdown. "I'm in the shower," she called out over the splattering of hot water pounding down around her.

"I'm going home," Laura called back. "Have fun with the queen bee today. Call me when you get back?"

"I will." Or maybe she wouldn't. It all depended on what happened when Brynn and Cassidy got behind closed doors together, and how badly Brynn reacted to their private time.

She lathered her shampoo and ran it through her chin-length, cotton-candy-colored hair, massaged it into her scalp, then let the water wash the suds away. The headache that had been developing since she rolled off the beanbag started to subside, and suddenly, everything seemed to clear. Cassidy wasn't her friend and never would be. Cassidy wasn't the ticket to her popularity, because Cassidy would never be seen in public with her. This had nothing to do with social status and everything to do with making a good grade on an English project. And that little epiphany would make working with Cassidy so much easier, or at least, Brynn hoped it would.

After drying off and spraying on so much body spray she could barely breathe before dressing, Brynn dried and styled her hair, then put on a little makeup. Nothing over the top, just enough to put a lock on the whole cute factor Brynn was aiming for. A dusting of pink over the eyes. Pink on the lips. A soft pink on the cheeks. Good grief, she looked like a big pink cotton ball.

Shoulders rounding, she let out a sigh. Brynn really needed Laura there to tell her she looked fine, but she wouldn't have dared to let Laura see her getting all dolled up for a study session with Cassidy Rivers. No doubt, that would be the nail in the proverbial coffin of their dying friendship. Yes. Dying. Laura never bailed first thing on a Saturday morning. They always… *always* had breakfast together, then usually went to the mall or the movies or the local skatepark or something. But not this morning.

Guess Laura didn't want to hang around for the "I'll catch up with you later because I would rather hang out with our biggest enemy" speech.

Brynn tore out of the bathroom and started down the hallway, not watching where she was going. She would've collided with her mother had Mommy Dearest not reached out to grab Brynn's arms before the two of them fell like bowling pins after a perfect strike.

"Where are you going in such a hurry?" her mother asked.

"I, um… I… class project with Cassidy Rivers."

"Cassidy Rivers?"

"Yes, ma'am."

"All dressed up like that?" Her mother settled her hands on her hips and gave Brynn one straight-through-the-soul stare down. It was her third-degree interrogation stance, the way she looked every time she wanted to break Brynn down.

"Well, we, um… might go to the mall or something."

"Brynn Michaels."

"What, Mom?" Brynn crossed her arms over her chest.

"What's really going on?"

"That's the truth."

"Then I'm sure you won't mind me calling Mrs. Rivers."

"Mom!"

"Brynn."

"Please don't embarrass me."

Awkward silence filled the narrow hallway, turning the air almost smothering. Brynn had the urge to fidget as her mother kept her weighty stare focused on Brynn, but she didn't move. No need to make her mother more suspicious.

"Fine," her mom finally said. "But I expect you to be home by seven for dinner."

"What if we get started on the project?"

"Then I expect a call from you, and you'd better be at Cassidy's house when you call."

"Fine," Brynn said in a huff. "When have I ever lied about where I'm going?"

"Never, and I'd like to keep it that way."

Brynn turned her head and rolled her eyes as her mom walked past her and continued down the hallway. She understood her mother's suspicion, she really did. But Brynn really was as honest as the day was long. She'd never lied to her mom, not over anything important. Brynn also never hung out with the likes of Cassidy Rivers and her clique of vapid, popular, spoiled little rich kids. It made sense for her mom to question their relationship now.

Relationship. There was that word again.

Chapter 8

"I'M WALKING over so I should be there in a bit." That was the last thing Cassidy heard Brynn say before hanging up the phone. The moment she tossed her iPhone onto her bed after ending the call, she went into frantic crazy mode.

Her room was perfectly clean as it always was, everything neat and in its place. But she wanted to hide all the superficial crap she was usually so proud of—like all her cheer trophies and the beauty pageant awards adorning her walls, dating back to when she was a little over two years old. Suddenly, everything in her room seemed like a lie. One big lie that Brynn would see right past. Or worse, she would buy into it all like everyone else did and wouldn't care to see the person beneath all the sparkling tiaras and golden pom-pom trophies.

Cassidy knew Brynn lived in the same neighborhood, but from their conversation, she'd learned Brynn's house was just around the corner and down the block. If she was walking, then that didn't give Cassidy much time to redesign her entire bedroom, so she put priority in the way she looked. Earlier, she had opted for a baby-blue Hollister T-shirt and some jean shorts. Now the brand name embroidered in big, white letters across her chest bothered her. Jeez, she looked like a billboard.

Bolting over to her large, walk-in closet, she quickly tossed the doors open and flicked the light on, gaze darting over to the racks and racks of tops all neatly organized by designer or brand, and in order by color. She shed the Hollister shirt then threw it across the closet and into her hamper. It wasn't dirty, but she didn't have the time to hang it back up on its corresponding hanger. A quick glance at her watch told her that her time was rapidly running out, and she huffed out a frustrated breath. Everything had a label. Everything was designer. Everything had a brand name.

Ugh! In all her years, she never would have thought finding something to dress *down* in would be so difficult. But she wanted to do this for Brynn. Basing her thoughts on the possibility the girl might be uncomfortable with brand names or designer clothing, she wanted to make her feel as comfortable as possible.

Finally, she found a white Victoria's Secret T-shirt that just had the word "Pink" across the front with little pink rhinestones. It made her smile as she pulled it on, since Brynn's hair was the same soft shade of pink.

When she traded her Armani Exchange jean shorts for a pair of True Religion jeans with a few tears across the front of the thighs, she felt a bit better. The jeans looked good on her. They were something she'd bought for a party once and ended up never wearing them because her friends had all decided to go in dresses instead. Lord knows why she left them forgotten in her closet, but she thanked everything in the clouds for having found them now. They had the same rocker feel Brynn exuded so easily.

One last time, she stopped in front of the floor-to-ceiling mirror inside her closet. *Yes, Brynn should be okay with this,* she thought, smoothing a hand down the front of the shirt.

The doorbell rang just as she exited her closet. She slammed the doors shut and darted down the stairs as if someone had lit a fire in those rocker jeans of hers.

Luckily, her mom had been okay with leaving her at home. Well, she'd complained about it at first, but Cassidy had dramatically explained that if she didn't work on this project, she would fail her class and it would drastically impact her final grade, thus ruining her chances to get into a good college and potentially creating a snowball effect that would have Cassidy living at home with her seventeen cats. Her mom understood and went to the mall with Nana without her. That actually gave Cassidy most of the day alone with Brynn, since her grandmother tried on no less than ten pairs of sandals at the Birkenstock store, fourteen bras at Macy's, and usually stopped to eat at least twice. Nana was a sucker for those freshly baked cookies and the bourbon chicken at the food court.

Standing in front of the door, she released a deep, meditative breath as she clasped her hand around the elaborately scrolled handle. For the life of her, she couldn't figure out why she was so nervous, but she was.

Here we go....

The door opened to reveal Brynn, standing on the front porch with the California sunshine highlighting the pink shades of her hair. Her bow-shaped lips were tinted with a light pink gloss, and her eyes were accented with the softest, palest pink shadow. Her outfit was considerably less gothic than her usual garb. The short skirt she wore revealed a patch of flawless, creamy skin between the hem and the tops of her knee-high socks, and the Mary Jane shoes she had chosen really tied her ensemble together. She looked almost innocent, bathed in sunlight and dressed in such a schoolgirl-type getup.

Beautiful, Cassidy almost blurted out loud.

Catching herself, she opened the door a bit wider, smiled, and said, "Hey, Brynn. Come in." She suddenly felt a bit underdressed in comparison to Brynn's perfectly put-together outfit. Well, the tables sure had turned quickly, hadn't they? It was normally Cassidy who was over accessorized and done up head to toe.

Funny, that.

"Thanks," Brynn said softly, hugging herself as she eased by. Cassidy caught a whiff of jasmine in the breeze. That girl smelled so freakin' good. Cassidy had just begun to lose herself in the scent when the sound of Brynn's voice pulled her back. "Mom wants me home by seven... unless we get caught up in the project."

"That's okay," she replied, closing and locking the door behind her. "Are you hungry? Wanna eat something first? Thirsty or something?" Cassidy Rivers, Suzy Homemaker extraordinaire. Not quite, since she really didn't know how to cook much, but she could play hostess. Pointing to the kitchen, she kept the smile plastered on her face. Not that she could wipe it away if she tried.

"I, um... I could use something to drink, I guess."

Cassidy sprung into action. "Come this way," she said before leading Brynn past the living room just off to the side of the airy, sunlit kitchen. "We have water, juices, most types of diet sodas, and almond milk."

"Diet Coke is cool, if you got it."

"Yep, sure do." Cassidy quickly fished a Diet Coke from the fridge and handed it to Brynn, trying not to enjoy the way Brynn's fingers brushed against hers for the briefest of moments in the exchange.

"Thank you," Brynn nearly whispered, as if she had lost her voice or something. Her cheeks turned a rosier red.

"So I was thinking—" Cassidy cleared her throat, shifting nervously from one foot to the other. "—we could work in my room, since there's an iPod hook up for the stereo system and a table we can spread all our stuff out on...."

"That's—"

"Um, if that's cool with you," she quickly added, cutting off Brynn's words.

"Your bedroom is fine."

"Great, follow me. It's right up the stairs, and there's a bathroom in my room if you need to go or whatever." Eww. Why had she just said that? How utterly freaky. The day was seemingly full of surprises. Hoping Brynn wouldn't think she was trying to perv on her while she peed or something, she turned on her heels and headed up the stairs to her room with the heat of a blush burning her cheeks and Brynn in tow.

Once inside her preppy, typical A-list bedroom, she felt her cheeks burn even hotter. This was the part she had almost feared. Having Brynn take one look at the decor in her room and automatically label her as something she really was not. The moment of truth, it seemed, had arrived. "Um… so this is my room."

"God, you really are a beauty queen," Brynn mumbled, wide eyes scoping the bedroom.

"Those are actually kinda old," Cassidy explained, feeling the temperature rising in her cheeks. "I was ten the last time I was in a pageant."

"I, um… didn't mean anything by it. I just—"

"Don't judge me for it, 'kay?"

"I wasn't, I…." Brynn sighed, lowering her crystal-blue stare. She was obviously chewing on the inside of her cheek, and Cassidy almost kicked herself for making Brynn feel the way she obviously did. "I just didn't know you were actually a beauty queen. I mean, we've made jokes about it. I just didn't know it was true."

"You make jokes about me being a beauty queen?" Cassidy asked, unsure if she should be mad or if that was actually kind of funny.

"Well, I, um… we…." Brynn bit down on her bottom lip, brows furrowed as she frowned. "Yeah, we do… or did. I mean, I won't joke anymore. It was just—"

"Whatever, it is what it is." Cassidy dismissively waffled her hand in the air.

"I'm really sorry, Cassidy. I didn't mean anything by it."

"Hey, at least you're not kissing my ass like everyone else. Whatevs."

Cassidy watched closely as Brynn set her backpack down on the floor, then reached in to fish out a book or something. The way Brynn knelt down, her skirt rose high up her thighs. Obviously, Brynn wasn't used to wearing outfits like that, and had Cassidy not been so mesmerized by so much of Brynn's skin showing, she might've laughed.

"So, I brought my notes from class," Brynn said as she returned to her feet. Cassidy quickly looked away so she wouldn't get caught ogling Brynn's goodies. "I think our first book has to be a classic novel by a California native."

"How about John Steinbeck? He's a classic, California-born author." With her breathing returning to normal after Brynn's unintentional indecent exposure, she walked over to the bookcase taking up nearly half the side of one of her walls. "I think I have some of his stuff here, if you haven't read—"

"*Of Mice and Men* is my fave!" Brynn blurted—eyes widened, lips curling into a smile so huge it made her entire face glow. "Can we do that one?"

"Sure, we can do that. I was gonna suggest either that or *Grapes of Wrath*. You like Steinbeck, huh?" It was clear she did. Brynn was all but beaming at the mention of the author, and her enthusiasm was a tad contagious. It elicited a soft, half-cocked smile from Cassidy.

"Honestly, I love Steinbeck." Brynn paused, glowing smile morphing into a subtle frown. "I'm sorry, Cass, but I'm surprised you know who he is."

Cassidy's smile died like a fading sunset. She didn't know what bugged her more, the fact that Brynn insulted her intellect, or that she'd called her "Cass." Definitely the latter.

"Please don't shorten my name. Only my dad calls me Cass...."

"I'm sorry. I didn't know it was a big deal. It just kinda happened. I won't do it again."

"It's just that he took off and left my mom and me for some chick in New York. He doesn't even call anymore, but he loves the floozy's kids as if they were his."

Why did she just blurt all that out? Since her dad had left them last year, she hadn't told anyone what really happened. Her friends thought he was always away on business, and that was the way she preferred it since it wasn't anyone's business anyway. In the interest of trying to show Brynn the real Cassidy, she left it alone and didn't bother to cover up her words or distract Brynn with something else.

Humility was something she was quickly coming to terms with.

"Then again, maybe if someone else calls me 'Cass' then it won't bug me as much... yanno?" A softer side to Cassidy Rivers. Oprah, prepare your couch.

She felt something warm and soft at her wrist, and the gentleness of it made her look down. What she found was something she'd never expected to see. It was Brynn's hand, reaching down for hers.

Cassidy froze. For a moment, it felt like her heart stopped beating. She didn't know what to say or how to react, so she simply didn't move. And apparently, her lack of reaction meant something entirely different to Brynn, because the girl didn't waste a second yanking her hand back and saying a soft, "Sorry."

"No, don't be sorry." Why was she sorry? She was nice and compassionate and tender and... real. In comparison to any one of Cassidy's dozens of friends, who all would have consoled her to her face before running back to the group to gossip about the news behind her back. "I've never said that to anyone. I guess I just didn't know how to react to nice... ness."

"It was a natural reaction." Brynn laughed. There was a nervous quiver to her voice and a new redness in her cheeks, which Cassidy found to be absolutely adorable.

"Your cheeks match your hair. It's cute," she blurted out, soft laughter matching Brynn's.

"So, I'm cute, huh?"

Dun dun dun. The moment had arrived. Now was not the time to be shy. Cassidy was a whole lot of things, but shy had never been one of them. "Yeah, you are. But don't tell anyone I said that, 'kay? Last thing I need is a bunch of snobby cheerleaders calling me a lezzie."

And they both laughed off the moment as if it had never happened.

Chapter 9

YES, Brynn laughed, but there was a whole lot more going on inside her head—curiosity, confusion, fear, and then the most oddly comfortable feeling she'd ever experienced. Cassidy Rivers called her cute.

Holy crap!

They sat close to each other, going over the scavenger hunt questions for the book they'd chosen. Brynn just knew Mrs. Miller would be impressed. *Of Mice and Men* was probably one of the best classic American novels ever, and thankfully, they'd both read it, so answering the questions was a breeze. But finishing the first part of the assignment left Brynn with about three extra hours to kill, and she really didn't want to leave Cassidy's house yet. Dare she admit she actually enjoyed Cassidy's company?

"So, um—" Brynn stood from the chair and closed her laptop. "—I guess we're finished, huh?"

Cassidy closed her own laptop, set it off to the side, and stood along with Brynn. "I guess so, but it's still early. You don't have to go yet, if you don't wanna."

"I don't," Brynn blurted, then immediately clamped her mouth shut. "I mean…." Oh, screw it. She put her foot in her mouth and couldn't take it back now.

"So then, don't. We can watch a movie or go hang out at the park or something."

"I thought you didn't want to be seen in public with me."

Cassidy had the decency to look embarrassed. Her gaze dropped momentarily, cerulean eyes hooding as she obviously collected and carefully arranged her response. "Yeah, well, they won't question me anyways. No one has the balls to."

Yeah. Maybe. But that didn't change the fact Cassidy had made it very clear she didn't want anyone seeing them together. While Brynn loved the idea of hanging out with Cassidy in public, where people could see that someone like Cassidy Rivers didn't consider Brynn an embarrassment, Brynn didn't want to be some kind of charity case. She wanted Cassidy to truly like hanging out with her.

"We can stay here. It's okay," Brynn finally said.

When Cassidy lifted her head again, determination shone in her cobalt stare. The words her gaze silently spoke, however, didn't quite make it past her lips. Instead, she shrugged casually and gave a short nod. "That's cool too."

Brynn dropped her backpack down in the chair again. This wasn't going to be like watching movies with Laura. There wasn't going to be any comfortable quiet and casual jokes about crappy dialogue or horrible acting. Brynn just didn't have that kind of calm, peaceful feeling with Cassidy, even though she wanted to.

She looked around the room for a stack of DVDs and didn't see any. There was no comfortable beanbag. In fact, the clothes Brynn had on wouldn't allow her to get much comfort at all, and now, looking at Cassidy's T-shirt and jeans, Brynn wished she'd dressed down too. Not that it mattered now. She was stuck.

"So, um… what kind of movies do you have?"

"I don't have movies. I have Netflix," Cassidy casually explained.

"Oh. We use Netflix too. It's just, when Laura and I watch movies, they're always DVDs," she offered, but Cassidy seemed unimpressed as she turned toward the nightstand next to her bed and picked up the remote.

The huge flat screen mounted to her wall came to life, and immediately, the bright red Netflix logo appeared. Cassidy flopped down onto one edge of her big bed, then scooted off to the side, leaving plenty of room for Brynn to join her. But Brynn didn't assume Cassidy wanted her that close, in such an intimate position. After all, a girl's bed was sacred, wasn't it? A place reserved for only the people she really cared about? At least it was to Brynn, and the very reason why only Laura had ever lay down in hers.

But then Cassidy patted the empty spot beside her and gave a Brynn a warm smile. She was actually offering Brynn a place to sit… on the bed… right beside her. Suddenly, Brynn's mouth felt drier than sand, and no amount of licking her lips made it any better.

Cautiously, she sat down on the edge, kicked off her Mary Janes, then relaxed a safe distance away from Cassidy. "So what do you want to watch?" she asked, hoping her complete nervousness didn't come out in the tremble of her voice.

"Isn't this your speed?" Cassidy quipped, nodding toward the TV.

A long list of horror movie covers ran from edge to edge—the likes of *Saw* and *Friday the 13th* and *Nightmare on Elm Street*, even movies Brynn had never heard of, with covers gory enough to make her cringe.

"Um, no." Brynn playfully grabbed the remote from Cassidy's hand, then scrolled up to the romantic comedies. The cursor landed on *Legally Blonde*, and Brynn laughed. "And this is yours, right?"

"No," Cassidy said flatly, taking the remote back.

As she scrolled through the unending supply of movies, Brynn stared at the screen, but she wasn't really watching any of the covers or titles. They were unimportant—cannon fodder, something to keep her eyes busy so she wouldn't accidentally start staring at Cassidy.

"This is it!" Cassidy all but yelped, waving the remote at the TV.

"*Wild Things*, huh?"

The bed shook as she gave an excited little bounce. Brynn shook away her daze so she could get a glimpse of what Cassidy was so damn excited about. The smile on Cassidy's face was nearly contagious, and the lilt in her voice as she said, "This is my favorite movie," made Brynn equally as excited to watch it.

"I've never seen it," Brynn quietly admitted.

"Shut up!" Cassidy gasped.

"What?"

"No. I didn't... I meant, you're kidding, right?"

"No."

"Oh my God! It's so good. And if my mother caught me watching this, she would kill me."

"Then we'll rebel against parental authority," Brynn said as she leaned over, reached across Cassidy's arm, and hit the play button. She looked up in time to catch Cassidy staring down at her with the softest gaze, like Cassidy had suddenly become as high as a kite. Brynn pulled back and cleared her throat, then settled into her spot a safe distance from Cassidy.

The opening scene started to play. The music was dark and sort of seductive. It immediately grabbed Brynn's attention. Ironically enough, both Brynn and Cassidy almost mirror imaged the two lead girls. One was Gothic and the other a rich, snobby, popular blonde. Only Brynn didn't grow up in a swampy trailer in the middle of Florida. She came from class, just like Cassidy did.

The movie dragged on, and Brynn thoroughly enjoyed it, even with all its darkness, violence, and taboo behavior. Then it came to a part that both fascinated and scared the hell out of her. The two girls, Suzie and Kelly were having a threesome with their skeevy guidance counselor. Brynn didn't really focus on him, but more on the girls. They were beautiful, bodies supple and softly glowing in the low light.

Freaked out by her immediate attraction to the girls, she quickly closed her eyes and looked away and prayed Cassidy didn't notice. She hoped the heat in her face didn't turn her cheeks blazing red, and for a moment, she silently debated telling Cassidy she needed to go.

But God help her, she wasn't ready to leave.

When the scene ended, she looked back up at the screen and everything seemed safe enough to watch, though the content was far outside anything Brynn would've considered decent. If her mom and dad caught her watching such filth, they would ground her for life and probably never let her visit Cassidy again.

Everything was as okay as Brynn thought it could be. She quietly sat beside Cassidy, watching the movie she'd picked. Everything was fine, and then the two girls kissed. For some stupid reason, Brynn pictured her and Cassidy on that screen—lips locked, bodies pressed together. Her mouth became dry again, and her heart beat a little harder. She suddenly became all too aware of Cassidy sitting beside her, the smell of her perfume and the sound of her soft breaths.

Brynn pushed up from the bed and said, "I have to go."

"But the movie—"

"I shouldn't be watching this."

"Oh c'mon. No one will know."

"I can't. I… I gotta go."

And before Cassidy could argue with her, Brynn grabbed her backpack and tore out of Cassidy's bedroom as if the devil were nipping at her heels. She raced out into the suburban evening, slamming Cassidy's front door behind her, and didn't stop running until her foot hit her driveway.

Home. At last. Ironically, though, she missed sitting beside Cassidy already.

The feelings running through her gave her cause for alarm, even though things suddenly made so much more sense now—why school dances were so lame, why Valentine's Day didn't matter as much to her as it did everyone else, why she hadn't ever tried to get a boyfriend. Brynn thought she'd had too many other things on her mind, that dating simply wasn't important. How wrong she'd been.

Dating was important.

Dating boys wasn't.

Her backpack slipped from her shoulder as she sank down on the driveway and pulled her bare legs up to her chest, trying not to burst into tears. The black schoolgirl skirt ruffled out around her. It was then that she noticed she'd bolted away from Cassidy's house so quickly, she'd left her adorable black Mary Janes behind.

Chapter 10

BRYNN bolted, and Cassidy remained on her bed long after the sound of the slamming door reverberated through the silent house. The movie kept playing, scenes continued to flash across the screen, and eventually the ending credits began to scroll upward, bathing her darkened room in dim light.

None of it mattered. Cassidy's thoughts were racing, and her emotions were beginning to get the best of her. Right up to the minute Brynn took off, Cassidy had been stupidly hoping that Brynn was feeling the same way she was. She thought she'd seen Brynn stealing glances at her, gaze wandering from the action on the flat screen and possibly wondering what it would be like if they acted out the scenes in real life. For a second, she had even talked herself into believing Brynn wanted to kiss her.

All that hope and possibility darted out behind Brynn, leaving Cassidy full of questions and worse, self-doubt—something she was not comfortable with *at all*. Why did Brynn leave? Was Brynn homophobic? She had been fine up until the girls in the movie kissed. Did Brynn think Cassidy was some sort of perv for wanting to watch such a sultry flick? Was she going to run off to school and spread vicious rumors about Cassidy's obvious comfort with lesbians, implying that she was into girls? It wasn't a lie, but it really wasn't what Cassidy needed, either.

The TV flickered before it returned to the main Netflix menu, and still she sat there with nothing but a headful of doubt and an uneasy feeling pulling at her stomach until her mom's voice cut through the silence, startling her. "Cassidy, honey? We're home. Come say hi to Nana," her mother called up from the spot at the base of the stairs where she always stood to make announcements Cassidy needed to hear beyond her always-closed bedroom door.

"Just a minute, Mom," she replied with a despondent sigh.

Reaching over for the remote, something black on the floor caught her attention. Brynn's cute Mary Janes. Jesus tap-dancing Christ, the girl had been so distraught she left without her shoes. That added a whole new level of insecurity to Cassidy's already mounting incertitude. *Am I really so bad that she couldn't wait to get away from me?* And there she thought Brynn had been genuinely enjoying her company, just as she had been thoroughly enjoying Brynn's.

Guess not.

She thought about taking Brynn's shoes back to her, but decided against it. Not only did she not really know which house was Brynn's since they all looked alike, but she didn't want to seem like a desperate stalker, checking up on the girl who had just rocketed out of her house because obviously she thought Cassidy was a freak.

So this is what she feels like at school. How horrible.

It was a feeling Cassidy didn't want to experience again.

Picking up the shoes, she allowed herself a moment to feel the supple leather—to take in the feel of the only thing she had of Brynn's—before she put them into her backpack so she could return them to her at school on Monday.

With the last trace of Brynn gone, she padded down the stairs and sat with her mother and grandmother in the kitchen while they made dinner. The rest of the evening was spent talking over food about her school activities, her grandmother's adventures in composting, and her mother's newfound love of gardening. Through all the chatter, Cassidy kept her wrist close to her face. The spot where Brynn's hand had delicately wrapped around it—warmly, caringly—when Cassidy told her about her father. It was stupid, but she felt close to Brynn that way. Why she even wanted to feel close to a girl who obviously didn't feel the same way about her was even stupider, but she did it anyway.

By the time everyone in the house agreed on plans for the following day and went to bed, Cassidy still hadn't shaken Brynn, or the way Brynn had reacted, from her system. She lay awake for hours, looking out the open window at the night sky, wondering for the millionth time why Brynn had taken off like a bat outta hell. She finally fell asleep with a clouded head and her wrist tucked tightly against her chest.

She awoke the same way too. The morning sun peered in past the sheer curtains, warming her face with its gentle rays. The aroma of toast and coffee lingered in the air, replacing the last, faint trace of Brynn's scent from her room.

What did it mean when your last thoughts of the night and first thoughts of the day were of the same person? Nothing good, that much was sure. Not when said person didn't feel the same way she did, nor did it appear that Brynn was even into playing for the same team she did. Talk about a whole other league. Brynn wasn't just outside the league, she was in a whole different ballpark, playing a totally different game altogether... and that just made Cassidy want her even more. Chalk it up to her competitive nature and her determined attitude.

She finally let go of the wrist she'd been clinging to all night long and rose from the bed, ready to face a day without Brynn Michaels padding through her head.

That mentality lasted all of maybe two hours.

Her grandmother and mom decided to change their plans and head out to the beach instead, since the day was too beautiful to pass up the opportunity. It was just another cloudless, sunny day in California to Cassidy, but to the women, it was a chance to soak in the sun and ocean breeze. Of course, she couldn't talk her way out of the beach. She tried, though. It didn't work and she now sat on the sand, clad in her white and black polka dot bikini and staring out at the shoreline in a daze.

A group of pretty girls gathered nearby—five of them, all perfectly tanned and sculpted in designer bikinis—four blondes and a ginger. They caught Cassidy's attention not because they were pretty, nor because their swimsuits were killer, but because the ginger chick sat sort of on the outside of the group of blondes. Even though they appeared to all be friends, the redhead didn't participate as actively in the conversation the others were engaged in. Her bikini was cut a different way—not the standard Brazilian style the others had, but a more covering bottom piece and a top with a flattering empire cut. The way she tucked her shoulder-length crimson hair behind one ear reminded Cassidy of Brynn. Hell, her whole demeanor was all Brynn.

Cassidy wanted to go and talk to her. She could always use a new friend, right? Exactly.

Excusing herself from her present company, she padded through the warm sand toward the group of girls. The four blondes all rose, almost synchronously, and headed toward the water before she even made it to the edge of their towels. The ginger, however, remained behind and smiled warmly up at her when Cassidy offered a friendly "Hello."

"Hi," the ginger replied, still smiling.

"I was sitting over there and noticed your bathing suit. It's great."

"Oh, thanks. I got it at Ross for twenty bucks. It's a Vivienne Westwood."

Was that right? What the heck was Ross and why hadn't Cassidy ever been there? A designer bathing suit for twenty dollars! What had she been missing? The surprised look on her face must have amused the ginger, because a giggle bubbled up past her lips, and she extended an arm. "I'm Natasha."

Cassidy reached down and placed her dainty palm in Natasha's hand, smiling from ear to ear suddenly. "That's a beautiful name. I'm Cassidy. Nice to meet you."

"Ditto."

Before Cassidy could get any further in conversation, one of the blondes called her newfound friend into the water, and Natasha politely excused herself. "My girlfriend apparently wants me to go swim or play chicken—" She giggled. Again. "But check out Ross whenever you get a chance."

"Will do. Thanks."

Natasha rose from her spot on the towel and ran off, kicking up sand as she crossed the beach before splashing into the water, leaving Cassidy to return to her mother and grandmother whom were in a deep discussion about the president. Cassidy knew that particular conversation would last quite some time since her grandmother was a die-hard Republican and her mother was the poster child for Democrats. At least it kept her mind off Brynn.

That was, until she thought about *not* thinking about Brynn, which led her to thinking about Brynn again. Which she did for the remainder of her stay at the beach, their stop at a Mexican place to eat dinner, all through the drive home, and well into the night as they pulled into the driveway, then through her shower, and as she got ready for bed.

This was becoming a pattern, it seemed. Going to bed with thoughts of Brynn darting out the door with no rhyme or reason, followed by feelings of insecurity and self-doubt, and finally, back to Brynn with more unanswered questions.

The worst part was that she couldn't even confront Brynn about why she'd booked it. Actually, she *could* ask Brynn, but she wouldn't out of fear of the answer. It was one thing to think you were a freak for liking girls; it was a-whole-nother to hear it said out loud by the one girl you had somehow begun to fall for.

And round and round her thoughts went until she resolved to remove Brynn from her head and try to get some sleep, knowing full well she dreaded facing the girl tomorrow more than she dreaded being outed at school.

Chapter 11

THE alarm clock wailed the most horrendous, biting sound and ripped Brynn from her sleep. She swatted at the thing, sending it flying off her nightstand and bouncing down to the floor. This was going to end up being the worst Monday ever. She could already feel it in the pit of her gut. Not only had she managed to get about two hours of sleep for all her internal panicking, but she also had to face Cassidy Rivers again—the reason for her internal panicking.

Groaning, Brynn rolled out of the bed. Her black fuzzy socks contrasted the light-gray carpeted floor. She kept staring down, only occasionally attempting to blink the sleep from her eyes. Yes, she absolutely *was* procrastinating, only because she didn't know what seeing Cassidy again would do to her.

Jeez, maybe she could suddenly become deathly ill and "call in sick" like her parents did when they didn't want to go to work. Wait. No. She couldn't. There was a stupid history quiz today.

Sighing, Brynn pushed up from the bed and went over to her closet. She grabbed a pair of black skinny jeans and a black hoodie, a black T-shirt, and her black Converse. Maybe if she looked like a shadow and hid beneath the cover of a hooded sweatshirt, Cassidy wouldn't notice her and wouldn't demand to know why she'd hightailed it out of the house. After all, it wasn't like she could tell Cassidy how she'd been picturing them in that movie instead of Neve and Denise.

After pulling her jeans up her short, skinny legs and the T-shirt and hoodie over her head, she slipped her feet into her shoes, then hurried down to the bathroom. The minutes were dwindling, and her stubborn reluctance to leave her bed had cost her precious moments in front of the mirror. Thankfully, her hair was still a bit damp from the shower last night, so she could brush it board straight without using the flatiron. Didn't matter really, though, since she fully intended to keep her entire head hidden under her hoodie.

"I'm gone, Mom," she called from the base of the stairs as she grabbed her backpack from the spot she'd dropped it Saturday evening.

Crazy thing was, she'd gone all weekend without touching her laptop. In fact, she hadn't even bothered with her phone—something that was normally glued to her hand at all times. Not this time. She spent Sunday hiding in the bed, beneath layers of covers so no one would bother her, all the while thinking about Cassidy and how she'd had the urge to kiss the cheerleader. Not once, but many, many times. That revelation scared the hell out of her and confused her. Did her desire to kiss Cassidy make her a lesbian?

Shaking off the thought as best as she could, she climbed into her car, eased out of the driveway, rounded the cul-de-sac, and headed out of her neighborhood. She tried not to stare as she passed the Riverses' house, tried not to wonder what Cassidy thought of her now.

The drive to school didn't take long at all. In fact, it didn't give Brynn a whole lot of time to think about anything, which was both good and bad. She didn't have a lot of time to stress over the unwavering need to taste Cassidy's lips or the unnerving uncertainty of facing the cheerleader for the first time. Would she blurt her feelings out because she always had those foot-in-mouth moments when she got nervous? Or would she be too afraid to utter the first word?

When Brynn pulled into the school's parking lot, the place was pretty much deserted. Brynn couldn't have been more relieved. She just knew she would be able to sneak into the library and wait out the thirty minutes to go before the bell rang. But the moment she climbed out of her car, grabbed her backpack from the passenger seat, and spun back around toward the school, Cassidy's sporty silver Scion wheeled in beside her. The sight of it stole Brynn's breath away. And when Cassidy popped up from the driver's side, Brynn instinctually lowered her head.

"I brought your shoes," Cassidy said, without a "Good morning" or even a hello. She rounded the back of her car, reached into her Dolce & Gabbana backpack, and pulled Brynn's Mary Janes out but didn't hand them to her. She just stood there, sort of hanging onto the shoes.

"Sorry for leaving them," Brynn responded, closing the distance between them. She reached out to grab her shoes, intent on doing it very quickly, but the moment her fingers grazed Cassidy's, Brynn froze. A gasp left her lips, and her eyes widened. She tried to swallow the new knot in her throat and couldn't. Nor could she bring herself to let go.

"Yeah, I get it. Don't worry, it won't happen again. I'd hate to make you rush out of my room because you're too homophobic to deal with a little chick-on-chick action."

"I'm not a homophobe!"

"Right. And I'm not blonde."

"Really, I'm not," Brynn's voice softened as she lowered her head. "That's, um… not why I left."

"You don't have to make excuses. It is what it is, I guess."

"You don't understand. You… you just… I…."

"No, you're right. I don't understand, so why don't you explain why you left like that?"

Brynn tucked her Mary Janes tight against her chest, hugging them to her body. The trembling in her hands became obvious. The knot in her throat tightened, and if her heart pounded any harder she swore it would explode in her chest.

"Cassidy," she whispered, fighting to raise her head and look the object of her newfound affection in the eyes. How in the hell was she supposed to admit how she felt? "I… I… I'm scared."

"Oh, so I scare you now? Thanks, Brynn." Cassidy turned on her heels and began to stalk away, blonde tresses flowing behind her like a platinum cape.

"Not you!" Brynn cried out in desperation. "I'm scared of me...."

Cassidy remained oblivious, walking farther away.

Tears began to brew in Brynn's eyes. She didn't know what to say to Cassidy to make her understand. Honestly, she didn't understand herself. One thing was certain; she hated watching Cassidy walk away from her like that. And as bad as she wanted to run after her, she didn't trust her legs not to send her tumbling to the ground.

Chapter 12

FIRST, second, third, and fourth periods all went by in one single, monotonous string of nothingness. By the time lunch rolled around, Cassidy had given up on trying to pay attention to her classes, friends, or even the music pouring through her earphones. She sat at her usual table, surrounded by the usual friends—cheerleaders, a few other A-list chicks who shared as close to her status as they could, and a couple of varsity football players who always hung out with the girls because they dated two of them.

The conversation was as it always was—other people. Who wore what, who dated who, who had been seen over the weekend doing stuff they'd never be caught doing, blah blah blah. She turned Mazzy Star up as loud as her iPod would go and kept picking at her chicken apple salad, attempting to completely drown out even the faintest hints of the chatter going on around her.

She was too busy looking around for Brynn to answer whatever dumb question Jenna had just asked her. Her little pink-headed fantasy was nowhere to be found. Brynn's weirdo friend, Laura, sat off to a side, purple head tucked behind a book. She was probably none too happy about being left alone to suffer the awkwardness of socializing. Heaven forbid she get up and talk to someone.

It dawned on her that not too long ago at all, she'd regarded Brynn with the same attitude. Just two days ago, as a matter of fact, she had walked by the same table where Laura now sat, barely acknowledging Brynn Michaels because she was just another freak. And now she was ready to all but scour the school for the girl.

Oh, how the mighty had fallen.

Somehow she managed to finish lunch without having to talk to anyone. Not that her friends hadn't noticed there was something wrong with her, but they weren't the type to ask. More than likely because they really didn't care; they just wanted the gossip. Since Cassidy wasn't offering any ante, they probably figured it wasn't worth their time to pry, so she made it to her fifth period economics class without anyone in her face.

It was actually rather peaceful. She kinda liked being alone, but it wouldn't last. It never did.

That point was painfully proven by the time she got to her locker after acing her economics pop quiz. Jenna came bounding over, bleached blonde hair bouncing around her cardigan. "So... you gonna tell me why you're so quiet?"

"Nope."

"Cassidy, what's wrong? You know you can talk to me about anything, right?"

Yeah, so you can go tell the rest of the school, right? "I'm fine." She couldn't pull her books out of her locker fast enough.

Jenna huffed, clearly agitated by Cassidy's lack of speech. "But Cassidy—"

"Just stop, okay? Leave me alone. I'm *fine.*" The red, metal door of Cassidy's locker slammed shut, the sound accentuating the end of her sentence. Jenna finally got the message. Or so she hoped. Either way, she wasn't about to stand around a moment longer. "I'll catch you at practice," Cassidy mumbled before trudging off down the long hallway to Mrs. Miller's classroom.

Reaching the door, she greeted the teacher, who stood to the side, posted like one of those weird British soldiers with the fuzzy hats who didn't move.

Cassidy made her way inside and intended on heading toward the back to her usual desk. Yeah, that's what she should have done. Instead, she saw the desk beside Brynn's empty, and for one reason or another, which she might never comprehend, she plopped into the seat and set her backpack down on the floor at her feet. When she looked up, not only was Brynn staring at her wide-eyed, but Laura had ambled into the classroom and was shooting daggers at her with those freaky zombie-type contact lenses she insisted on wearing, because obviously, she didn't think she looked enough like a whack job already.

Cassidy smiled oh-so-sweetly in return. Laura seethed, and Brynn's eyes widened even more as she sank down into her seat. For a moment there, she had been so wrapped up in what was going on with Brynn, she'd forgotten she could totally use her bitch card, which she happily waved in the air at Laura.

The freak growled at her as she passed her by, opting to take another seat instead of fighting Cassidy for the one she'd claimed for the day. "Relax, spaz. You can have your seat back tomorrow. No need to growl like a dog."

Brynn didn't look at all too happy with her choice of words toward her friend, but Cassidy had had all she could handle of Brynn's rejection for one day. Locking her gaze with Brynn's, she whispered softly enough so Brynn could hear, but the rest of the kids couldn't. "What did you mean this morning?"

"Is this really a good time to have this conversation?" Brynn whispered back, keeping her eyes straight ahead.

"I don't see why not. It's not like we're talking about drugs or illegal crap. It was a movie, for the love of all things holy."

"I shouldn't have been watching it."

"Shouldn't have or didn't want to?"

"Shouldn't have." Brynn finally looked over, meeting Cassidy's stare with an intensity she'd never seen from the shy emo girl before. "It made me think about… things, okay?"

"And whatever you thought about made you bolt from my house without so much as a good-bye or an explanation?" Cassidy's pale brows shot up as Brynn's cheeks turned a bright shade of crimson.

Oh. Is she trying to say what I think she's trying to say?

Cassidy shifted in her seat, suddenly uncomfortable with the uncertainty of the moment. God, it was like pulling teeth with this chick. Why couldn't Brynn just say what was on her mind instead of making her play the guessing game? What if she got it wrong? Read the signals wrong? That would end in even more embarrassment, and she couldn't have that, so she leaned in even more and whispered, "I think I get it, but can you kindly elaborate?"

"Cassidy...."

Brynn chewed the inside of her cheek and averted her eyes again. Her chest rose and fell a little too quickly. Her cheeks flushed brighter red. She opened her mouth to speak, and Cassidy hung onto the moment, but the moment was foiled by Mrs. Miller calling the class to attention.

"Later... please," Brynn breathed without looking over.

And just like that, Cassidy was right back to wondering what the hell had happened.

To make matters worse, she was seated at the front of the class for the remainder of the period, which subjected her to Mrs. Miller's annoying, nasal voice as she read through not one, not two, but three chapters in a book. To add insult to *that* injury, she threw in a little quiz at the end for good measure. It would have been torturous save for the little moments when Cassidy would catch Brynn stealing glances at her through that ever-present part in her bangs.

Those moments made sitting at the front of the class completely worth it. Like a dork, Cassidy would smile in return each time she caught Brynn's eyes. Instead of smiling, Brynn looked like a mouse who'd been caught stealing cheese and would sink down into her seat again, only to casually glance her way a few minutes later. They played that game of smiling and ducking until the bell mercifully rang.

Chapter 13

FOR some stupid reason, Brynn had it in her mind that Cassidy would follow her out to the parking lot, where they would talk about things and maybe come to some sort of... well, something about Brynn's feelings. Maybe that was too much to hope for, because the moment the bell rang, one of Cassidy's vapid, narcissistic, bottle-blonde friends grabbed Cassidy and dragged her out of the classroom, going on about cheerleading practice.

An intense wave of disappointment rolled over Brynn. She honestly wanted to have that conversation with Cassidy, though why, she didn't know. Surely Cassidy would belittle her and make fun of her, probably call her names and laugh in her face, because that's what Cassidy and all her A-list friends did.

Maybe this is a mistake.

Cassidy and her friends headed in one direction; Brynn headed in the other. She was almost to her locker when she felt someone run up beside her. Reluctantly, Brynn turned her head and she found her bestie glaring at her.

"I didn't ask her to sit there," Brynn said, before Laura had a chance to tear into her about Cassidy stealing the spot Laura sat in all year.

"You didn't tell her to move either," Laura quickly retorted, which stopped Brynn dead in her tracks.

"You're the one who said we didn't need to make waves! What? Did you expect me to argue with her over your seat? Why didn't you argue with her?"

"Excuse me for expecting my best friend to take up for me!"

Just as Brynn opened her mouth to respond, Laura spun on her heels and stalked away. Twice that had happened to her today, and frankly, it was getting old.

"Ugh!" Brynn growled, stomping her Converse against the linoleum. She shook her head and continued toward her locker, mind going right back to Cassidy and the mounting disappointment of not being able to talk about things or, at the very least, see the cheerleader again.

She spun the lock around and around, not really paying attention to the numbers. And when the locker didn't immediately open, her anger grew ten times more intense. She almost wanted to put her fist straight through the metal door, but Brynn didn't have that type of temper. She was a pacifist.

Shoulders rounded, she sighed and took a step back. This was getting her absolutely nowhere fast.

One last try got her into her locker. She switched out the books in her backpack for the ones she needed to do her homework tonight, then closed the door and spun the lock again. She hefted her backpack up to her shoulders, took a deep breath and slowly let it go, then headed toward the stairwell and out of the school.

The moment she reached the chain-link fencing, she spotted Cassidy in front of the line, commanding the cheerleaders as they did their routines. She'd changed into these spandex-looking red pants and a white Majestic Hills High T-shirt, and she still looked as beautiful as she had in her regular clothes. Even from beyond the fence, Brynn could see the outline of the muscles in Cassidy's legs, and the T-shirt caressed her slender body in such a way it accented her breasts.

Jeez, to have boobs like that, Brynn thought as she frowned down at her hidden cleavage.

Brynn curled her fingers in the fencing and pressed her face to the chain-link. She was staring, completely mesmerized, and watching the cheerleader in an almost stalkerish fashion. And yet, she couldn't bring herself to leave, even when Cassidy spotted her.

Her body tensed when Cassidy turned to the rest of the girls and shook her head. She then went over to the bleachers and grabbed a red MHHS duffle bag. But when Cassidy pushed through the gate and headed Brynn's way, Brynn stopped breathing… if only for a moment.

"Hey," Cassidy called from a few feet away.

Brynn stepped back from the fence, fighting to avert her stare. "I didn't mean to stare, I… I just…."

"It's okay. I like you watching me."

"You do?" Brynn frowned. Her feet immediately stopped shuffling.

"Yeah, I do…."

"I, um… that talk. Did you…? I mean, we could go somewhere where your friends won't see us."

"If you want to. I'm okay with sitting on the bleachers, but if you prefer somewhere else, lead the way." Cassidy waved one arm in one direction and the other toward the bleachers.

"Maybe we could go back to our cars. I don't want any trouble started for you, and if they see you talking to me…."

Cassidy shrugged indifferently. "Meh, they're already drilling me about my seating change in last period, but okay, let's head back to the cars."

Brynn wrapped both hands around the straps of her backpack, white-knuckling them as she walked beside the one person she couldn't seem to get out of her head. She kept her eyes trained on the green grass beneath their feet. They walked over the yard and down the hill in the direction of the high school parking lot, keeping completely quiet until Brynn said in a low, barely audible, trembling voice, "I haven't stopped thinking about you since I left your house."

"Now, is that because you left me sitting there"—Cassidy stopped walking for a moment before continuing—"or because of something else about me?"

Brynn's feet abruptly halted. She chewed the inside of her cheek for a long while, considering whether it was safe to tell Cassidy how she really felt, or if she needed to keep it a dark and dirty secret.

"Cassidy," she said, slowly turning her head. "I thought about you because... because I feel these things I don't understand. Those feelings, they... they scare me."

IF EVER anyone was the poster child for realization, Cassidy Rivers was at that moment the very embodiment. She hadn't even realized Brynn had stopped walking until she herself came to a halt. She blinked a few times, as if her eyelids had any connection to her brain's function. When she opened her mouth to speak, Brynn interrupted the thousands of possible things she was prepared to say by whispering a sad, pleading, "Please don't make fun of me."

Make fun of her? Was she kidding? That was the last thing on Cassidy's mind. She smiled crookedly, almost sinisterly if it were to be labeled at all. Her intention, however, was nowhere near malicious. "That's why you left? 'Cause you like me? Like, *like* me, like me?"

"I guess. I don't know. I... I...." Brynn exhaled raggedly and dropped her stare to the ground again. "I'm confused. I mean... I like you, but I...."

"But you're confused about the capacity in which you like me," Cassidy finished for her, forming more of a statement than a question.

"I suppose. I've never imagined kissing anyone before, then... that movie, and... and you, and... I pictured.... It freaked me out, so I ran away." Brynn's head bolted straight up, and she locked eyes with Cassidy. She had that kill-me-now look on her face. "Oh my God, please don't tell anyone about this. I totally don't even know why I told you. I mean, you asked. I didn't want you mad at me. If your friends find out…," she urgently rambled.

Cassidy stood in place, probably seeming absolutely mad, and not in the angry sense. Her face hurt from smiling. The heavens opened. Angels sang and she all but dropped to her knees to thank everything holy for the fact that not only was she not crazy, but she'd been right.

"Chillax. I like you too," she said softly, still smiling at poor Brynn, who looked like she wanted the earth to swallow her whole. "I wanted you to stay because I like you. I wanted you to hang out, 'cause I like you, and it hurt when you left… 'cause I like you. Get it now?"

"Like… *like* me, like me? Seriously?"

"Is there an echo in this parking lot?" Cassidy laughed. "Yes, like *like* you, like you."

"So you're not going to gossip about me to your skeevy friends?"

"Nope. I won't even gossip about you to the non-skeevy ones."

They both laughed, and finally, Brynn seemed to relax. Her pink lips curled into a genuine smile, one that made those adorable dimples appear in her rosy cheeks. She licked those totally kissable lips, then said, "I still don't know what I'm doing or what I'm feeling. I just know I wanted to kiss you, and I swear to God, I didn't want to leave your house, but I was so freaked out, I didn't know what else to do."

Cassidy glanced in the direction of the field a ways away, where every cheerleader on the squad had stopped their practice and now stood facing her and Brynn. Oh, she could hear them talking now. Thing was, though, somewhere along the line, Cassidy stopped giving a crap about what anyone else had to say about her. The only opinion that mattered was that of the girl who stood in front of her. So, to really give the "prep" squad something to talk about, she draped one arm around Brynn's shoulders and led her toward their cars, turning their backs on the cheerleaders, whom Cassidy could swear she heard gasp collectively.

"I don't know what I'm doing either, but I know I like you and I know you like me. We'll figure it out, right?"

"I would like that."

"Good, 'cause you've got about four months of being stuck with me."

"'Stuck' isn't exactly the word I would use. You're only 'stuck' when you're somewhere you don't want to be."

As they neared their side-by-side cars, Cassidy stopped at the rear of her Scion and turned Brynn to face her. Cassidy bit her own lip, fighting off the urge to kiss Brynn. The only reason she didn't was because Brynn had probably been through enough emotional ups and downs through the day to last her two lifetimes. Instead of pressing her mouth to Brynn's and sampling whatever nuance of Brynn Michaels she could, Cassidy offered her one last, brilliant smile. "So call me, maybe?"

Brynn rolled her eyes. "Really? I mean, of all songs under the sun...."

Cassidy laughed and shrugged. "What? I *am* a cheerleader. It's, like, standard for us."

"I won't hold that against you."

"Feel free to hold anything else against me," Cassidy replied with a salacious smirk before clicking the little alarm on her keys and sliding in behind the wheel.

Chapter 14

IT DIDN'T take a whole lot of self-convincing to make Brynn pick up the phone and call Cassidy later that night. They spent hours talking, and honestly, it felt like a few precious minutes. They mostly laughed and talked about things they both liked to do. They talked about school and how everyone had their little secrets. In fact, it seemed like everyone at that school had a deep, dark, dirty little secret.

Brynn suggested, and Cassidy reluctantly agreed, that keeping their friendship on the down-low wasn't a bad idea for right now, at least until Brynn felt a little more comfortable with what was going on inside her and where her life was so obviously heading. No need to make matters worse when things were already so weird for her.

They talked until Brynn's father tapped his meaty knuckle against her bedroom door and ordered in his best captain's voice, "Lights out, kiddo."

Brynn and Cassidy said their good-byes. They promised to talk tomorrow, which they did through fun little texts sent on the sly, or those few and far between moments when they managed to sneak away from their normal crowds.

That became their routine over the course of the week. They both stuck to their own friends, casually stealing quick glances of each other whenever they could, careful so no one would see them. Then, the moment they got home at night, one called the other, or Brynn walked down to Cassidy's house just to hang out on the old tree swing from Cassidy's youth. They wasted a few nights watching movies, but never once did they kiss, despite Brynn's constant urges to lean in and steal a quick taste.

The more Brynn hung out with Cassidy, the more she wanted to be around her. Cassidy's laughter was contagious. Her smile was intoxicating. Her sense of humor made everything wrong in the world go away, and Brynn couldn't get enough of it, even to the point of neglecting her best friend, Laura, who grew more and more distant as the week wore on.

The two times Laura had called, Brynn told her she couldn't talk right now, that she had homework or things to do with her mother— little white lies, only because she didn't feel like she could tell Laura the truth. The truth. Very simply put, she was starting to fall hard for someone she never thought she could even like.

Friday night came, and Cassidy had some sort of game she had to cheer for. They wouldn't be able to see each other until Cassidy got home, which was well after Brynn's curfew. It was Laura and Brynn's normal movie night anyway, and cancelling on her BFF probably wouldn't have been a good idea at that point. When Laura got angry, truly angry, she got pretty vicious, and the last thing Brynn needed was someone she'd once trusted with every secret she ever had hating her.

After supper was finished, Brynn went straight up to her room. The only window she had overlooked the driveway, and had she somehow managed to miss the sound of blaring music and squealing tires, she would've seen Laura's little import whipping into the driveway. A minute later, she heard the car door slam and the pounding of tiny feet jogging up the stairs.

"Totally thought you would bail on me," Laura said as she closed the bedroom door behind her. There was a teasing lilt to her voice, playful, though Brynn knew Laura meant no humor in what she'd said.

"Why? We've always hung out on Fridays."

"I know. You just haven't really been around lately."

"Yes I have."

"Well, physically"—Laura plopped down on the bed and began untying her black combat boots—"but not mentally."

What could Brynn say? It was true. She hadn't been there much because her mind and heart seemed to be following Cassidy around. Not that she could tell Laura any of that. She quickly searched for a comeback, and the best excuse she could think of was, "It's school. I'm just trying to focus so I can make a good grade."

"I understand."

No, Laura really didn't.

Brynn grabbed a movie from the stack Laura had left last week. They hadn't made it through all of them, and there were still a few Brynn really wanted to see—one being *Girl, Interrupted*. She'd only seen bits and pieces of it in the past, but she'd read the book and knew the story well.

As the opening credits began to roll, she settled into the beanbag, foregoing the normal popcorn and sodas. Laura didn't mention it. Brynn kept her phone right beside her, set on silent, just in case Cassidy decided to text. She really hoped Cassidy would send her a text. That was all she could think about, even as a movie she'd been dying to see played right in front of her face.

The screen on her phone lit up and immediately caught Brynn's attention. When she looked down, she saw a new message from Cassidy. It said *I would soooo rather be with you right now.* The message made her smile. It made that warm little rush she got every time she talked to Cassidy blossom in her chest.

The message she sent back read *I wish you were here too.*

After she responded, she tucked her phone against her chest—screen down so the light wouldn't interrupt the movie and she could feel the vibration if Cassidy chose to respond. It took a few minutes, but Cassidy eventually came back. *What'cha doin'? I'm in a locker room full of sweaty, stinky cheerleaders. Ick. >.<*

The silly face Cassidy sent back with her text made Brynn laugh, and apparently the sound pulled Laura's attention away from the movie. She turned a questioning eye at Brynn.

"Sorry," Brynn mouthed as she responded to Cassidy's text. *Thought that was your kinda thing. LOL!!!*

As if! Halftime means I get to sit and bask in their ickiness. Sooooo not hot at ALL!

I'll bet you're sexy when you're all hot and sweaty. Brynn blushed and immediately hit the send button before she lost the courage to go through with the message. The moment the bar across the screen read "sent," she wished she could take it back. It was meant to be nothing but playful, only it sounded so very bad.

It took a while to receive Cassidy's reply, but when she did, there wasn't just a message, but a picture as well. The image depicted Cassidy, crimson MHHS cheer uniform top visibly drenched in sweat and her pulled-back hair flying out from the sides as if she'd been in a wind tunnel. The text said, *Yeah, about as sexy as Princess Fiona when she's in ogre mode.*

You're still beautiful.

You need your eyes examined, but thank you. <3

<3 Can we hang out tomorrow? I really want to see you.

For sure. Bank on it. What are you finally doing tonight? Is Wednesday Addams at your place?

Laura? Yes. I think she's glaring at me. Hard to tell in the dark.

Uh-oh. Be careful. She might get pissy and decide to sacrifice you to Satan.

Brynn was just about to respond when she heard the remote control hit the floor right beside her. The bed springs squeaked, and the lights came on. Laura had her arms crossed over her chest, and her glare focused on Brynn.

"Who the hell are you talking to?" she said, voice angry and demanding.

"No one."

"You sure are texting a lot for someone who isn't talking to anyone. Now what's going on that you can't even watch one movie with me?"

"Nothing. I'll stop, I swear." Brynn pushed up from the beanbag, dropping her phone in the process. Laura managed to swoop down and grab it before Brynn could hide what she'd been doing. "Give me my phone," she said, holding out her hand.

"Tell me who you were talking to."

Under normal circumstances, Brynn would've told Laura anything she wanted to know. Under normal circumstances, she wouldn't have hidden anything from Laura in the first place. But these weren't normal circumstances, and frankly, it wasn't Laura's business.

"No. Now give me my phone."

Smirking, Laura pressed the little round button, and the screen lit up. Brynn knew the string of messages would be right there waiting and Laura would see the way Cassidy talked about her and how Brynn hadn't taken up for her. Those messages had the potential to end their friendship… what was left of it, anyway.

Brynn dove forward, reaching out to clamp her hand around her phone. They both tumbled to the ground. The phone tumbled across the room, smacking the wall before landing on the floor. Laura pushed Brynn off her and made Brynn hit the desk. The thuds and booms were getting ridiculous, and Brynn knew if she didn't get a handle on things, her mom and dad would soon come pounding up the stairs.

"Get out of my house!" Brynn growled as she rose to her feet. "You had no right to do that."

"What are you hiding from me?"

"Obviously, it's none of your business."

"If that's how you feel…."

"It is."

"Fine!"

"Fine!"

Laura grabbed her backpack from the floor where she'd dropped it, stormed out of the bedroom, and down the stairs. Brynn immediately went after her phone, but when she found it, it wouldn't turn back on, and she couldn't respond to Cassidy's text. Brynn's heart sank. Laura had just killed her lifeline to the only person who truly made Brynn happy these days.

Chapter 15

THE game was over, with Majestic Hills beating Westwood High by a landslide. Cassidy made her way back to the girls' locker room, where she went to the duffle bag she kept inside the red locker reserved for the captain of the cheer squad. Fishing her phone out from the side pocket, her lips tightened into a frown when she saw Brynn still hadn't responded to her last text. After sending it, she'd waited for a reply for as long as she could before heading back out for the third quarter. When Brynn didn't reply right away, Cassidy chalked it up to her being busy with Laura and maybe not having had a chance to get back to her. But more than enough time had passed by now, and Brynn wasn't the type to keep her waiting.

Maybe my text offended her.... It was, after all, Brynn's best friend Cassidy had been talking about. But by now, she thought Brynn had grown used to her casual joking. She did take a jab at Laura whenever possible, but come on, it was so hard not to. The girl was a basket case.

She slid her finger across the touch screen to unlock her phone, then sent Brynn another message before heading out to her car.

Hey, I'm sorry if I offended you with my last comment. It was only a joke. Holla back, 'kay? <3

All the way home, down the winding, curvy roads of the San Fernando Valley, all through the suburban streets and into the neighborhood of Majestic Hills, Cassidy kept glancing at her phone in anticipation of Brynn's reply. When she pulled up to the house and cut the engine, there were still no notifications on the screen.

She seriously thought about heading over to Brynn's house to find out if she was okay. It didn't sit well with her that she might have offended Brynn so much she hadn't responded. Or worse, something could have happened. Something terrible, like Laura having seen their texting banter and really sacrificed Brynn to Satan. Really, that wasn't a probability… but it remained a slight possibility. The chick was downright creeptastic.

A glance back down at the phone told her it was a little past eleven o'clock. It was way too late to knock on Brynn's door now, even if she did brave going over to the Michaelses' household.

Maybe she fell asleep.

Maybe she's having fun with her friend.

Maybe her friend butchered her to pieces.

Gah! She had to get out of the car and into the house before she scared herself silly and ended up at Brynn's doorstep, time be damned. Besides, she was really, really sweaty and needed a shower, like, yesterday.

One would think a good hour and a half later, after Cassidy showered, shaved her legs, washed her hair and blow dried it, moisturized her skin, and exfoliated her face, Brynn would have replied. But when Cassidy checked her phone, there were still no new messages, save for a mass text from their cheer coach commending all the girls for such a great job at the game earlier.

Did Cassidy want to look like an obsessed freak and risk texting Brynn one last time? God, it would be pretty embarrassing if she had just fallen asleep early and woke up tomorrow to a gajillion texts from Cassidy acting like an overprotective lover. *Oprah, call Dr. Phil.*

Screw it. Despite her better judgment, she sent one more text message.

Brynnie, please holla back when you get this message. I really am sorry. Have a good night and I'll see you tomorrow. Hopefully. <3 <3

She added an extra heart and tapped her finger over the "send" button just as there was a soft rap on her door. "Cassidy? Are you still awake, honey?" her mom asked, voice gentle, tone sleepy.

"Yeah, Mom. Come in."

Cassidy's mother padded into the room, white satin robe flowing around her body like an ethereal angel. Cassidy never did understand why her dad left her mom—a vision of beauty—for the cheap trick he now called his wife. Her mom was everything that lady wasn't. Where the skeeze was short and pudgy in all the wrong places, her mother was tall, elegant, and had curves as sleek as a Porsche, even though she had slightly higher mileage. The skeeze had stringy hair, which she dyed blonde, and dark eyebrows that gave away her real hair color. Miranda's hair was long, thick, and naturally straight, with a hue that resembled wheat fields in the sunshine. She had a vibrant laugh, and when she smiled, the whole room seemed to light up. The other lady sounded like Fran Drescher in a paper bag.

Really, what was her dad thinking?

"How'd the game go?" Her mom sat down at the foot of her bed, smoothing a hand over the white down comforter spread across the queen-size mattress.

"It was good. Majestic won forty-two to twelve."

"Oh, great. I take it you had fun as always?"

Was her mother really in her room past midnight to talk about high school football? "Yeah, it was fun. What's up, Mom?" Might as well cut to the chase and spare her mom the small talk. Not that Cassidy didn't appreciate it. Her mom always came in to check on her after the games, but Cassidy had other things on her mind that night. Namely, why Brynn *still* hadn't replied to her.

"Sweetie, with Nana in town for a while and you just having turned eighteen, we think it might be best for you to start setting aside some time so we can begin to help you control your powers."

Ugh, this again.

Every time Cassidy started to forget she came from a ridiculously long and prominent line of witches, the women in her family reminded her all over again of not only her lineage, but of the fact that she had powers she frankly didn't want or need.

The look on her face must have been one her mom had seen more often than not lately, because she gave Cassidy a sympathetic smile and said, "I know it's not on the top of your to-do list, but you really have to start learning the basics at the very least. It's for your own safety, Cassidy."

Cassidy opened her mouth to speak, but her mom just kept talking. She had the habit of doing that every now and then when it came to this particular subject, which was why Cassidy normally drowned her out or simply appeased her by agreeing to do it but never getting around to it.

"With your grandmother in town, there's so much you can learn. More than I can teach you, because her book of shadows is by far more complex than mine since I stopped practicing magic for your father." A momentary, wistful expression crossed her mother's delicate features, but it was gone by the start of her next sentence. "If you don't start getting a handle on the things you can do now, you're going to have a really hard time channeling your energies. Your power is at its peak right now, and it's only going to get stronger as the weeks go by. You can't risk having something happen in public that you're not prepared to handle…."

Yada, yada, freakin' yada. The *Charmed* talk kept going on, and Cassidy kept her eyes glued to the phone sitting on her nightstand, waiting, hoping, for the darn thing to light up with the message she'd been waiting for. If she could use a Vulcan mind meld on it, it would have reached Brynn by now.

"…so how about we get a start on it tomorrow?"

"Huh, what?" Definitely not tomorrow. She'd promised Brynn they'd hang out, and she wasn't about to ditch her Pinky for Witchcraft

101. "No, I can't do it tomorrow, I have a study sesh with Brynn for our big English project. Um, maybe Sunday, 'kay?" There. Her mom sighed and gave her a disapproving look, but she took what she could get and reluctantly nodded.

"Okay, sweetheart. We'll start on Sunday. It'll be fun, I promise," she said, rising from the bed to kiss Cassidy's temple.

"Yeah, fun. Can't wait."

"Listen, don't judge it until you've given it a chance. There's a lot your grandmother can show you." Miranda smiled again, and this time it was that radiant smile that could get her anything she wanted. "Have a good night, Cassidy. I love you."

"G'night, Mom. I love you too. Sweet dreams."

Her mother exited as gracefully as she'd entered, with the satiny fabric of her robe flowing behind her, top covered by waves of waist-length, honey-colored hair. When she closed the door behind her and Cassidy was left alone in her room again, she got ready for bed by removing all the extra pillows used only for decoration and turning off the lamp at her bedside.

With the room bathed in darkness, she nestled into her sheets, feeling the exhaustion of her day finally wear down on her. And still, she fought sleep until she could no longer, by keeping her gaze focused on the phone that never lit up with a message.

Chapter 16

AS SOON as the dawning sun cracked the barrier of Brynn's thick, purple curtains, she leapt from her bed and hurried down the stairs. The smell of cooked bacon, eggs, and homemade biscuits wafted out from the kitchen. She heard her father rustling the newspaper even before she darkened the door. He looked up, but not long enough to get much more than a glimpse.

"Morning, kiddo," he said.

"Morning, Daddy," she said, walking right by him and over to the fridge for a soda. "My phone won't turn on. I think I need a new one."

"Brynn Michaels!" her mother said in that *you're-in-big-trouble* tone of voice all mothers seemed to have. "That was a four-hundred-dollar phone. What happened?"

"Laura got mad at me and threw it across my bedroom last night... right before she stormed out of the house and slammed the front door."

The spatula in her mother's hand clanked against the pan. The newspaper her father had been reading folded. Both her parents looked at Brynn as if she'd grown a third eye in the center of her forehead, which truthfully, was a completely legitimate response to the news Brynn had just spilled. She and Laura almost never fought, not like that, anyway. They never got to the point of violence.

"What happened?" her father asked.

"I've told that girl about slamming doors," her mother said as she went back to cooking the eggs.

Brynn sank down in the chair across from her father. Really, all she'd wanted to do was tell them about the phone, then run as fast as she could to Cassidy's house, just in case Cassidy had tried to call or text or something. She didn't want to give the impression she was upset with her or anything, because nothing could be further from the truth.

"Brynn?" her father said, leaning his elbows against the table as he scrutinized her. "What happened?"

"She got mad at me because I was texting during the movie. I had the phone on silent. She just got mad."

"Who were you texting?"

Sighing, Brynn cut her eyes over to the door, wishing she could make a break for it before the interrogation got too bad. As many times as she'd come home in the past, complaining about Cassidy and her merry band of... um, witches or whatever, to ignore time with Laura simply to text Cassidy would surely stir up a few questions, questions she would have to answer or look guilty for doing something she had yet to do.

"Cassidy Rivers," she mumbled softly.

"Cassidy Rivers?" her parents asked in perfect harmony, surprise filling their voices.

"Yes." Brynn spun her can of soda between her thumb and forefinger. "Mrs. Miller is making us work together on a project." She shrugged. "Cass is actually being kinda cool now. I mean, she's not as mean as I thought. She's actually kinda nice."

"Nice enough to ignore your best friend?" her mother asked as she piled a tall helping of golden-yellow scrambled eggs onto Brynn's plate.

"I dunno," Brynn said, picking up her fork.

She aimlessly pushed the pile of eggs around as she stared at her plate. Truthfully, she felt bad for fighting with Laura, but the things she was going through, the feelings she had for Cassidy, weren't something she felt comfortable sharing with anyone right now, including her best friend.

"Are you going to eat or play with your food?" her father asked.

"I'm really not that hungry."

"Breakfast is important, kiddo. Eat half, okay?"

Swallowing, Brynn scooped up a forkful of fluffy scrambled eggs. She ate them, even though she really didn't want to, but she knew if she didn't, her parents would keep her at that table forever. Right now, she didn't think she could deal with that kind of torture. She wanted to see Cassidy… like yesterday.

Her plate was a little more than half clean, nothing left but a slice of bacon and half a biscuit, but that was enough to satisfy her mom and dad. They didn't tell her to stay there when she stood from the table and didn't ask her to wait for her little sister—the all-day sleeper—before being allowed to make her escape, which was a good thing, because as it stood, she was willing to forego a shower just to see Cassidy.

Immediately, Brynn went to the bathroom, took some minty fresh toothpaste to her breakfast breath, and scrubbed and scrubbed until her mouth felt clean. Then she brushed her hair back and finished it off with a black ribbon fashioned into a headband. She didn't bother with makeup, because makeup took way too long. Then she tore down the hall and into her bedroom.

As she dressed in her jeans and black, girlie T-shirt, she wondered if Cassidy was even awake yet or if all this rushing would be a complete waste of time. Most kids her age wouldn't dare to open their eyes at such an ungodly hour, but Brynn was on a mission.

She slipped her tiny feet into a pair of ratty black Converse, grabbed her hoodie, and then ripped down the stairs and out the front door before anyone could stop her.

It wasn't until she felt the cool morning air against her face and saw the golden sunlight rising on the horizon that Brynn actually slowed down to her normal pace. There was still dew on the grass. A few houses even had their porch lights on. Most of the neighbors still slept soundly, but Brynn didn't care, and she sure hoped Cassidy wasn't the type to sleep in on a Saturday either.

She rounded the corner, and the moment Cassidy's house came into view, a smile curled the corner of her lips. Brynn picked up the pace again, running full force for the Riverses' house. Her Converse flapped against the asphalt, all the way up the concrete walkway and straight to Cassidy's front door. When she lifted her arm to knock, her hand was trembling, and she realized she could barely breathe.

The door opened, and an incredibly beautiful woman with hair nearly as gold as the sun stood in the doorway. Her eyes were soft and kind. Her lips formed a sincere smile. The woman almost glowed, and with beauty like that, Brynn knew she had to be Cassidy's mom.

"I'm here to see Cassidy," Brynn said breathlessly.

"Oh, sweetie, she's still in—"

"I'm awake," Brynn heard Cassidy saying from somewhere far away, maybe even from the top of the stairs.

Cassidy's mom stepped out of the doorway and nodded for Brynn to come in. Brynn stepped in the foyer and saw the girl she couldn't stop thinking about, standing at the top of the stairs, still in a white camisole and a pair of silky-looking pink pajama bottoms. Her blonde hair was a bit tousled, and her eyes still had that hooded, sleepy look to them, but all Brynn saw was the most beautiful girl she'd ever met.

Brynn started up the stairs, holding the rail so she didn't fall on her face. "My phone is broken," she said at about the halfway point. "Laura broke it. It wouldn't turn on. I'm sorry if I missed any texts. My stupid phone…," she rambled on.

Cassidy's mom said something about fresh orange juice and waffles in the kitchen if the girls were hungry, to which Cassidy smiled and offered a "Thanks, Mom" before fixing her cerulean gaze on Brynn as she cleared the top step.

"I was worried that I offended you with my last text about Laura," she said, voice soft and still filled with sleep.

"No. You didn't. Laura wanted to know who I was texting, and when I refused to show her, she got mad. Anyway, my phone got bounced off the wall. I need to take it to the Apple store."

"That chick's a bi—" Cassidy caught herself, no doubt for Brynn's sake. "She's a... witch."

"She's just afraid of losing me, I think." Brynn stepped up to the landing, meeting Cassidy face-to-face, with nothing but a few inches of air between them. Her eyes hooded when she smiled and said a soft, "Hey there."

"Hey there, Pinky," Cassidy said before leaning in and pressing a soft kiss to Brynn's cheek. Her minty-fresh breath brushed over Brynn's skin when she said, "Wanna come sit in my room while I get ready for the day? I just have to do my hair and get dressed."

At the feel of Cassidy's soft lips to her warm cheek, Brynn's eyelids fluttered, and a smile curled her mouth. It was an innocent peck, a chaste... nothing, really. But God did Brynn wish it was more. When Cassidy pulled away, Brynn wanted to whimper, but she forced herself not to.

"Yeah, I can wait."

"Coolies, come on." Cassidy reached out to take Brynn's hand in hers, lacing their fingers together as she led her down the long hallway and to her bedroom, where she closed the door behind them. "Sit, get comfy. I'm gonna change real quick."

Unabashedly, she pulled her cami over her head and tossed it into a nearby laundry hamper before walking into her huge closet, completely topless.

Brynn's eyes nearly popped right out of their sockets. Cassidy didn't have a bra on, and that gave Brynn a clear shot of two particular parts of anatomy she'd found herself fantasizing about recently. And for the record, they were more beautiful than Brynn ever imagined.

That was the first time she'd seen Cassidy without a shirt on, and honestly, Cassidy's disappearing into the closet disappointed her. It was becoming incredibly hard for Brynn to deny the attraction she felt toward Cassidy, harder to lie and say she felt nothing. She wasn't sure how much longer she could hide behind an aloof and distant "she's just my study partner" in reference to Cassidy.

When Cassidy finally reappeared from behind the closet door, she had on a light blue American Eagle shirt that covered what Brynn had been so eager to see again. But Cassidy looked stunning as always, even in a T-shirt and jeans.

"I like that outfit," Brynn said softly.

Cassidy's azure eyes lit up suddenly. She looked like someone had just told her she'd been crowned *America's Next Top Model*. A slow, wicked smile tugged the edges of her pouty lips upward. "Oh my gawd, Brynnie! Lemme give you a makeover! I wanna see you in something other than black. Pleeeeeease?"

Chapter 17

CASSIDY ignored the reluctance and almost hint of hesitation in Brynn's softly whispered "okay." All she saw was a green light to get her Pinky in some clothes that complemented the curves she knew Brynn had.

Squealing with glee, she grabbed Brynn's hand and all but dragged her into the large California closet. There was more than enough room for both of them inside. Still smiling from ear to ear, she commanded Brynn to strip out of the black garb she wore. Okay, maybe, just maybe, there was more than one reason why she wanted to play dress-up with the emo object of her affection. She could admit to wanting to see all that supple, creamy skin Brynn always hid away beneath layers of dark clothing.

Cassidy was open enough with her sexuality and more than confident with her sensuality, but as Brynn stood there, doe-eyed and stammering to find words, Cassidy reminded herself that Brynn had probably never before been intimately almost nude around another girl. She just didn't see Laura the freak as an exhibitionist of any sort. As far as Cassidy knew, Brynn didn't have any other friends that were as close to her as Laura. So that pretty much narrowed this moment down to what was probably Brynn's first time being half-naked around another girl. *Thank goodness for cheerleading.* Locker rooms had taught her a long time ago how to be comfortable around barely dressed girls.

"Come on, Brynn. It's just me."

Brynn chewed her bottom lip so hard that where the pink skin of her mouth met her chin, the flesh turned a pale white. Her hands were obviously shaking as she slowly unzipped her hooded sweatshirt. "I, um." Brynn swallowed so hard, Cassidy couldn't help noticing the waving of her throat. "I've never changed clothes in front of anyone else."

"Yeah, I figured as much. But really, it's no big deal. I won't judge you," Cassidy said patiently.

"It's... I...."

Poor Brynn looked like she was living that nightmare where you're standing on a stage in nothing but underwear before all your peers. It was cute. "Would it make you more comfortable if I turned around?" Cassidy really didn't want to miss the opportunity to see her little Pinky's gorgeous body, but if it would make Brynn more comfortable with the situation, she would.

"Maybe. I don't know." Brynn sighed, then licked her clearly dry lips.

Cassidy turned around, giving Brynn some privacy. "Better?" She silently scowled at the sight before her. The plain, soft pink wall of her closet didn't boast nearly as much appeal as Brynn's body, but she would rather Brynn be comfortable than have her standing there trying to understand if she was turned on or freaked out. Chances were she was a little bit of both—a natural reaction for any girl who was just realizing she was into other girls. Cassidy had had her share of it. Brynn, again, probably not ever.

"You can turn around now," Brynn said, voice shaking.

When Cassidy turned back around, she found Brynn hugging her chest, obviously trying to cover as much of her body as her thin arms would. Her cheeks were bright red. Her legs were clamped together tightly, and her eyes were fixed on her bare, black-polished toes. Cassidy didn't see the awkwardness emanating from Brynn. All she could see was creamy skin and black jeans hugging gentle curves.

"Brynnie, you're beautiful. Quit covering yourself up." Cassidy reached out to take Brynn's hand, which was tucked tightly under her arm, pressing against her ribs. She led her to the large selection of tops, which ranged in nearly every color of the rainbow, except black. Tank tops, camisoles, T-shirts, and blouses all hung neatly beside one another for Brynn.

"What colors do you like?" Cassidy asked her, keeping her gaze forward on the clothing rack instead of looking at Brynn. It was difficult, but she resolved to make Brynn feel okay with the situation, even if not seeing the girl she dreamed about felt like slow torture.

"Black. Purple. Red."

"Purple. We can work with purple." They'd *have* to work with purple because Cassidy didn't have anything in black save for one T-shirt, and red looked horrible on her, so she loathed the color. She had all shades of purple, though, ranging from a light lilac to a rich, almost magenta color in a Marc Jacobs blouse.

The darker purple probably wouldn't complement Brynn's hair color as much as a soft lavender would, so she pulled out a few tops in lighter hues and laid them out on the chaise set against the wall to their left. If she could get Brynn covered up in a top, maybe she wouldn't feel so awkward anymore. "Do you like any of these?"

"Whatever you think'll look okay on me. I trust you."

Without hesitation, Cassidy swept up a light violet Abercrombie & Fitch tank top. It worked for Brynn because aside from a small "A&F" tag on the lower left hem, there weren't any large advertising letters across the front. She was trying to add color to Brynn, not change her style. She actually rather liked Brynn's somewhat layered look, but it needed a little softness. Handing the tank top over, again, she averted her gaze from anywhere in the vicinity of Brynn's chest. "We can pair that up with a darker purple gingham blouse I have and leave it open in the front," Cassidy said, more to herself than to Brynn, who took the tank top slowly before Cassidy returned to searching through the clothes hanging in her closest for the top she'd been talking about.

"Aha, found it."

"Does this look okay?" Brynn quietly asked, smoothing her hands over the lilac tank top now clinging to her flat stomach and subtle curves. "I mean, it feels nice, but do I look okay?"

"You look beautiful," Cassidy replied encouragingly, as she held the cotton blouse open for Brynn to slide her arms in. She took extra care in making sure the neckline was folded down neatly and the button hems were straight. Once she rolled the sleeves up to Brynn's elbows, she stood back and smiled. "I think some white jeans would work with that top combo." Cassidy wasted no time in turning around to the other side of the closet, where she pulled a pair of white denims from their respective hanger. When she returned to stand in front of Brynn, Pinky looked a little more at ease and a bit less like she was ready to faint. "See if these fit. My ass is bigger than yours, I think."

This time, Brynn immediately started slipping out of her jeans. She didn't seem anywhere near as nervous as she had been before. In fact, she seemed to be almost confident, even as her dark purple boy shorts became exposed to Cassidy's gaze.

Finally, the heavens awarded Cassidy's patience and good behavior by granting her a peek at Brynn's goods. So it wasn't her whole body, but the clothes she wore belied the rounded bottom she rocked. Where Brynn might blush profusely and look away if Cassidy's panty-covered butt was bared for her to see, Cassidy felt herself smiling and appreciating the hell out of the view.

"Maybe my ass isn't bigger after all."

"Huh? What?"

Brynn clumsily turned her head back and fell into a one-legged, jean-knotted half spin as she tried to get a view of what Cassidy was talking about. The move led to her falling forward enough that Cassidy had to catch her or she would've hit the floor hard.

"Sorry. Sorry," Brynn repeated as she tried to right herself again.

Cassidy was laughing too hard to really notice her arms around Brynn's lithe body. Only when both girls stood straight up again did she realize she hadn't let go of Brynn. She didn't want to, either. As a matter of fact, she pressed against her a little more, bringing Brynn in a bit tighter. Brynn's minty breath caressed Cassidy's face, making her want to suddenly taste the parted lips that were all but beckoning her. She wouldn't, though. Out of respect for Brynn and the fact that she was standing with one leg in the jeans and one out, panty-covered ass still exposed, Cassidy restrained herself and instead began to release her hold.

BRYNN never expected to find herself half-naked and in Cassidy's arms the way she was. She knew the day would come when they'd want to get a little closer, a little more intimate with each other. She had no idea when she'd crawled out of her bed this morning, today would be the day. With Cassidy's arms around her, and the closeness of their bodies, Brynn didn't want to stop whatever was about to happen between them. She both feared it and craved it. And the moment Cassidy's arms started to loosen, she felt like her chance to really see another side of Cassidy Rivers had passed.

"Don't," she whispered airily, dropping her gaze to Cassidy's lips.

"Are you on your feet?" Cassidy never ceased to surprise her. There they stood at the edge of their first intimate moment, and she was worried about Brynn falling over.

"As good as I can be."

"You sure? You can be pretty clumsy."

The moment Brynn opened her mouth to respond, Cassidy's lips locked with hers. This was it, the moment she'd been waiting for a whole week. For seven long days, she'd fantasized about what it would be like to finally kiss Cassidy Rivers. Would Brynn freak out? Would her kiss be clumsy like her? Or would it be soft and sweet like Cassidy? Would they do it once and never again? Or do it many, many more times.

As Cassidy eased her tongue through the slight part in Brynn's lips, Brynn closed her eyes and gave up on wondering where this might go. She gave into the feel of finally having their mouths touching in a not-so-chaste-sorta way. It was the first time anyone had ever kissed Brynn that way, the first experience she had with anything remotely sexual.

Cassidy's arms tightened, and Brynn returned the hug, splaying her fingers over Cassidy's back. They held each other tight, even as Cassidy slowly released her lips. Brynn couldn't bring herself to open her eyes, and she damn sure didn't want to let go of Cassidy's body.

"I don't get why people wanna come out of the closet. I rather like it in here," Cassidy said breathlessly.

"I kinda liked it myself," Brynn smiled. "We should, um"—heat flushed her cheeks—"do it again sometime. Maybe?"

"Oh yeah, we're definitely doing that again sometime soon. For now, pull your jeans up so we can get you over to the Apple store."

"And the frozen yogurt place," Brynn added as she reached down and pulled the jeans Cassidy loaned her up to her waist. Only Cassidy's fingers were the ones that ended up on the zipper.

Brynn watched curiously as Cassidy fastened the button, all the while wearing a silly smile on her face. She couldn't believe it had actually happened, that she'd actually kissed a girl… and liked it. It felt so right and so normal, some of that ridiculous fear she'd had before faded away.

Chapter 18

ONCE Cassidy had Brynn situated inside the confines of her Scion, she drove them to the nearby mall. She zoomed into a parking spot and wasted no time leading Brynn inside, directly to the Apple store so her Pinky could hopefully fix the phone her freak friend had broken. This was her lifeline to Brynn, the main way to communicate with her when they couldn't be together, so to say it was important to Cassidy to get that phone fixed as soon as like, yesterday, was an understatement.

Standing in the line for the Genius bar, Cassidy tapped her foot impatiently against the polished floor of the store and took the opportunity to ogle Brynn, who was still glowing from their kiss earlier. She wasn't the only one. Cassidy almost ran a stop sign and two red lights on her way there because she was absorbed in the moment inside her closet. It had been more than she'd ever imagined it to be, and she'd imagined the scenario countless times. Brynn's lips were pliant, her kiss tender and full of curiosity combined with excitement.

The look on her face must have given her thoughts away, because when Brynn's eyes met hers, Pinky smiled brightly and giggled softly.

"What?" Cassidy asked.

"Nothing." Brynn's smile widened. She was so obviously lying.

"Yeah, right. You look like the Cheshire Cat."

Brynn's cheeks turned that cute shade of bright red Cassidy adored, and when Pinky cut her eyes away, Cassidy knew she'd been caught in a little daydream.

"I've never kissed anyone the way we kissed," Brynn quietly admitted.

Well, that wasn't quite the same for Cassidy, who'd had a boy or two kiss her in the past. Nothing ever came of it, though, because Cassidy lost interest rather quickly. Before realizing she was into girls, she'd just thought boys were stupid and couldn't hold her attention. Now she knew better. Even still, with her two or three somewhat passionate kisses in the past, nothing compared to what she'd shared with Brynn less than an hour ago. Boys never gave her butterflies. Boys never made her eyes close when their lips touched, and boys certainly never ever managed to make her feel as exhilarated as Brynn had.

"I have, but it's never been as amazing or even half as toe-curling as that was. So it was kinda my first time too."

"Toe-curling? You, um… you thought it was toe-curling?"

"Well, yeah. My toes curled."

"I, um… I think mine did too." Brynn giggled softly. It was probably the cutest, most innocent sound Cassidy had ever heard. "Have you ever, um… you know?"

Oh man. That was a heavy question. There were so many implications that Brynn's "you know" could mean. Cassidy shook her head gently and cleared her throat. "Not really. I mean, a guy felt up my boob once, if that counts as something."

And she'd hated it. It felt wrong and dirty, so she'd immediately pulled her shirt down and left him sitting in his car while she went to catch a ride with one of the other cheerleaders. Eww. The memory made her skin crawl. Luckily, all it took was the thought of Brynn's hand over her girl globe instead to replace the near-vomit memory with hope and a smile.

"I've never had anyone like me enough to try," Brynn confessed.

The line moved forward, placing them next to be attended. Thank freakin' gawd. The importance of Brynn's cell phone could not be measured in words. Fixing her attention back to Pinky, Cassidy offered her a soft smile. "Well, I like you enough to try." Yeah, she said it. And what? It was worth watching that precious blush flower across Brynn's cheeks all over again.

"Can I help you?" the woman in blue behind the counter asked.

Brynn had to clear her throat before she spoke. "I, um"—the red in her cheeks glowed brighter—"my phone is busted. It won't come on."

"Is it under warranty?"

"Yes, ma'am."

"Well, you can leave it with us and come back in an hour or so. We'll see if we can't get it to boot. If not, we'll just replace it."

"Thank you," Brynn said as she handed over the phone. As soon as the woman behind the counter took the device, Brynn reached down and grabbed Cassidy's hand and started urging her out the door.

Cassidy happily followed Brynn out past the pretty Mac computers and into the mall's crowded hallway. She laced her fingers with Brynn's, glancing down to smile at the contrast of Brynn's silky porcelain skin tone against her own tanned flesh. When she looked up again, she was still smiling. God, she was doing a whole lot of that since Brynn had come into her life. Or stumbled in. Or fate via Mrs. Miller had delivered her. Whatever.

She gave Brynn's hand a little squeeze and was just about to lean over and press her lips to her cheek when she heard someone cry out, "Are you freakin' serious?"

Brynn immediately tensed. Her fingers tightened around Cassidy's, causing her fingertips to tingle from the pressure in her clasp. "Crap," Brynn hissed under her breath as she released Cassidy's hand like a hot potato.

There wasn't anything that could have ticked Cassidy off more than the purple-headed, black-clad freak who came charging toward them like that bat out of hell Ozzy Osbourne bit the head off of. *She* was the reason Brynn had just let go of her hand. *She* was the only person who stood between her and Pinky, and Cassidy loathed competition as much as she abhorred interference. At the moment, Laura represented both.

Brynn took a step forward and said, "Laura, it isn't what you—"

"You know what?" Laura interrupted. "I'm so sick of you lying all the time. You hate her!" She stabbed her pointy finger in Cassidy's direction. It took a whole lot of restraint for Cassidy not to break that lanky digit in two. "Now you're going all lezzie with her? What the hell?"

Brynn opened her mouth, but Cassidy stepped between them. No way in hell was anyone going to talk to her Pinky that way and get away with it.

"Jealous much? God, freak. Quit spazzing." Cassidy's tone was insulting. Downright demeaning. It was the cool, arrogant voice she reserved for the meanest of insults because she knew nothing bugged the crap out of people more than being treated like someone who wasn't even worth a raised tone. "What's your deal, anyway? Maybe you're the lesbian, what with the way you're all up in Brynn's Kool-Aid."

"You're freaking mental, Cassidy. Wait until everyone hears about you holding Brynn's hand. You just wait!"

"Oh, I'm cowering," Cassidy snorted. "Really? Who's gonna care that we were holding hands? More importantly, who's even gonna listen to you? You're a nobody."

"Stop!" Brynn yelled. Her face had blanched to a pale white, paler than her normal creamy porcelain. "Just stop." She looked at Cassidy and frowned, then looked back at Laura. "Why are you being so mean to me?"

"Oh, you haven't seen mean yet," Laura said. "How could you? She's the enemy."

"She's being nice to me."

"To your face, only because you guys have the project. She hates you, remember?"

Brynn lowered her head.

At this point, Cassidy clenched her hands into fists at her side.

Truth be told, she'd never really hated Brynn, just misunderstood her. Maybe even envied her casual attitude a bit too. For a moment she let Laura's words hit her. Just for a moment, though. She bounced right back and straight into bitch-face mode. She pointed one finger straight into Laura's black-hoodie-covered chest and laughed sardonically. "What would you know about who or what I hate? You don't know squat about anyone or anything because no—one—likes—you." With each enunciated word, she poked her finger harder and harder against the fabric covering Laura's chest. "Go ahead, psycho. Bring your A-game. By the time I'm done with you, you're gonna wish you were under that rock you slithered out from."

Malice. She had it in spades.

Laura growled as she stormed away, pushing between the two of them and shoving them both out of her way. When Cassidy looked over at Brynn, she saw genuine fear and maybe a little sadness in Brynn's eyes. If there was anything that could completely dissipate the fury she was feeling, it was the expression on Brynn's face.

Immediately, Cassidy's stance changed. She stepped back and sighed, offering Brynn an apologetic look before the words even made it past her lips. "I'm sorry" was all she could say. Knowing Brynn was caught in the middle between her crazy friend and her new… girlfriend? Girl who was a friend? Whatever, that was something she'd figure out later. All she knew now was that she'd probably made the situation worse, and not for her, but for Brynn, who still looked like she was caught somewhere between tears and anger. "I'm sorry," Cassidy repeated, offering Brynn her hand, if Brynn would even dare to touch her again.

"It's not your fault," Brynn said as she let Cassidy lace their fingers.

The moment they touched again, Cassidy felt heat build in her palm. She felt the rolling, frizzling, crackling of energy, and knew her emotions were pushing her powers and giving them the jolt they needed to burst to life and embarrass the hell out of her. She wondered if Brynn could feel it too.

"I'm just worried about what Laura is going to do," Brynn said as if she hadn't felt a thing.

Cassidy felt like the Wicked Witch of the West. If it hadn't been for her interrupting, Laura and Brynn might have hashed out whatever it was the freak was so bugged about. Since it was too late to do anything now, she did what she could. Looking Brynn straight in the eyes, she squared her shoulders and softly promised, "I won't let her do anything to you, 'kay?"

"I believe you," Brynn whispered, tightening her fingers around Cassidy's.

"Good." Cassidy nodded. "Now, you wanna walk over to the frozen yogurt place in the food court while we wait for your phone?"

"Is this a date?" Brynn finally smiled, which elicited a mirroring smile from Cassidy.

"This is anything you want it to be, Brynnie."

"I think I like the idea of this being a date."

Chapter 19

AS THEY headed through the crowds of happy, oblivious mall loiterers, Cassidy kept her hand locked around Brynn's. Not that Brynn minded. She actually liked the fact Cassidy accepted her enough to be seen in public with her. Maybe Brynn sounded desperate, but she didn't care. She'd always wondered what life with the in-crowd would be like and with Cassidy by her side, maybe one day she would find out… if Laura didn't ruin it for her first.

Sighing, she looked at the people passing by them—the happy families, the husbands and wives, the girlfriends and boyfriends holding hands. Brynn realized she saw no one like her and Cassidy, and she didn't mean two girls on such opposite ends of the spectrum there was no way they could possibly be friends. Rather two girls who felt so much for each other they *had* to hold hands.

Was it wrong, the way Cassidy touched her, the way they kissed, and how close they'd become? Would Laura turn them both into social lepers by outing them to the school? What was there to out? Did a single kiss make Brynn a lesbian?

They arrived at the yogurt place, and Brynn had been so lost in her own mind she hadn't heard the guy behind the counter ask her what she wanted and hadn't noticed Cassidy staring at her like she'd grown a second head. "I, um… vanilla. Large. With white chocolate chunks and nuts, please," Brynn said before absently moving to the side. She hadn't even noticed she was no longer holding Cassidy's hand.

"Small, fat-free chocolate, with sugar-free fudge and low-carb graham crackers, please," Cassidy chimed in after Brynn. She kept glancing over at Brynn with worry... or something... creasing her features. "You okay?" she asked softly as they moved down toward the register at the opposite end of the counter.

"I'm okay," Brynn lied as her stare scoured the crowd. She had a feeling Cassidy would notice she hadn't looked her in the eyes again, not since they'd started toward the food court. "You're not worried about everyone in the school thinking we're lesbians, are you?"

Cassidy shrugged one dainty shoulder in disregard. "Nah."

"You're not afraid of being bullied?" Brynn paused. "Wait, of course you're not. You've never been bullied, have you?"

"Um... no. But I know what it's like to be outside of a group because you're different and sometimes, that's just as bad."

"What group would consider *you* different enough to make you an outcast?"

Cassidy looked down at her white sandals. She seemed to be dissecting the polish on her toes by the way she stared so intently. It was the first time Brynn had ever seen her act anything other than confident. When she looked up again, her expression was soft, and if Brynn didn't know any better, she'd swear Cassidy was hurt.

"Let's just say not all the beauty pageant girls are nice, especially when you're prettier than they are."

"That sounds so life-ending." Brynn rolled her eyes. Only then did she realize how ugly that made her sound. "Sorry, I... I just.... You have no idea how hard it is having people make fun of you and stare at you. If Laura goes around telling them I'm a lesbian, then I'll really be made fun of. I'm already the 'emo freak'—add anything else to that and I might as well hide under a rock."

"Back to Laura again?" Cassidy huffed, clearly growing irritated by the mention of the many things Laura could do to ruin Brynn. "I *promise* you that no matter what she does, it'll get turned around on her, and she'll be the brunt of her own game. *This* I know how to do, so just trust me, 'kay?"

The guy behind the counter handed their order over on a bright pink tray. Cassidy grabbed it before Brynn had a chance to. Brynn picked up two plastic spoons and a pile of napkins, then followed Cassidy over to the tables. They both sat down, each girl reaching for her dessert. Brynn took a bite, then said, "I don't want anything bad for Laura. I just don't want her making trouble for me... or you."

"Brynnie," Cassidy sighed. "That girl is so far off anyone's radar she couldn't make trouble if she knew how to spell it. Chillax."

"'Chillax'. Got it."

After all, Cassidy had a point. Brynn needed to relax and stop letting Laura have so much power over her. On the one hand, she hated the wedge that had been shoved between her and her best friend. On the other, Cassidy gave her something, made her feel something she'd never experienced in her life. Cassidy gave her a new reason to be happy. Why couldn't Laura accept her happiness? Why couldn't Laura be happy for her?

"We should have a sleepover," Brynn blurted. Who knew where that idea came from?

"We totes should!"

"Can I spend the night at your place tonight? We can watch movies, and I promise not to bail on you."

Cassidy squealed. "Yay! Yes! Not just yes, heck yeah!"

"Would you mind coming over and meeting my parents? They have a thing about me spending the night with people they don't know. It's so stupid." Brynn rolled her eyes. "I mean, I'm almost eighteen already."

"No, not at all," Cassidy said as she licked chocolate frozen yogurt from her spoon. "Parents love me."

"My daddy is military, so make sure you do the whole 'sir' and 'ma'am' thing. It'll earn you mad points with them."

"Sir and ma'am are my specialty."

"Good." Brynn smiled wider as she scooped up more yogurt and plopped the spoon into her mouth. She licked away the gooey goodness, watching closely as Cassidy did the same.

As she watched the pink plastic spoon slip between Cassidy's pursed lips, she remembered the way those lips had felt on hers, the way they tasted like strawberry, and how soft they were as Cassidy kissed her. It made everything inside her all warm and fuzzy, just like she felt when Cassidy held her.

"I, um… I think I'm finished," Brynn said, clearing her throat.

The sound of a spoon scraping across the bottom of the bowl indicated Cassidy had finished her dessert as well. She took one final long, almost teasing lick of her spoon, clearing it of any remaining frosty yumminess, before dropping it into the empty Styrofoam bowl. "Me too."

"I guess we can pick up my phone and head to my house then?"

"Sounds like a plan, gorgeous."

Cassidy rose from her seat, the sound of the metal legs scraping across the linoleum floor of the crowded food court. She turned to walk away, leaving her bowl on the table for the mall maintenance staff to clean up, but when she saw Brynn begin to clear hers and place it atop the tray, she turned around again and followed suit.

With their trash in the receptacle, Cassidy once again reached out her hand for Brynn's, smiling when their fingers intertwined. Together, they made their way back to the Apple store, where Brynn was elated to discover the geniuses at the Genius bar hadn't been able to fix her phone, but they'd transferred all the data to a brand new phone, which they already had charged and waiting for her.

It seemed the little fiasco with Laura was beginning to ease away. As they made their way through the mall, Brynn didn't even stress that they were holding hands in public. As a matter of fact, she sorta liked the way it looked in the reflection of the windows they passed by. It was natural. Cute even, since they were about as far opposites as anyone could picture—even though people wouldn't know that from looking at her dressed in Cassidy's clothes. Which, she had to admit, looked pretty nice on her.

To her left, the bag holding the box to her new phone swung gently back and forth while to her right, Cassidy chattered on about how tacky the stuff at Claire's had gotten and how absolutely adorable the stuff at Sanrio was, even though she'd never be caught dead in public with anything Hello Kitty because it was soooo last year.

Outside, the sunshine warmed her shoulders while the breeze billowed by, caressing her cheeks. She felt good. Really, really good. The day had suddenly gotten so much better with the simple promise of sleeping over at Cassidy's house. It was her chance to make it up to Cassidy for darting out of her house that night. This time, not only would she not dart out, she might have to fight herself to not crawl into Cassidy's bed and snuggle into her.

The same cheerleader who'd given Brynn a new reason to smile suddenly screamed bloody murder, followed by a string of expletives. When she looked up, her eyes widened and her mouth fell open to form a big "O."

There, across the shiny silver side of Cassidy's car, the word "DYKE" was spray painted in black capital letters.

Cassidy kept cursing and Brynn silently kissed their good day together good-bye.

Chapter 20

AFTER that vulgar display of anger, Cassidy should've still been seething. But she wasn't. Not only was she not fuming, but she was plotting the devastating downfall of Laura Dorien. In her head, the elaborate plan spun like a spider's web, weaving out of control as she pulled out of the mall's parking lot and made her way back to Majestic Hills.

They rode in silence save for the radio playing softly. The music served more as background noise than entertainment or distraction. Cassidy simply couldn't be distracted. She was like a geek with a new science project, eagerly anticipating the steps she had to take to ensure the big shiny award at the end went to her while her competition wept in defeat. Oh yeah. Laura was going to regret ever becoming a blip on her radar, and she was definitely going to suffer extreme torment if she caused Brynn even an iota of pain or embarrassment.

Rounding the corner, she stopped the car in front of her house and turned to Brynn, who sat quietly looking out the window. "Do you mind if I park here and we walk over to your house? I don't want your parents asking about my car if they see it."

She didn't want Brynn to think Laura's little stunt had in any way ruined their plans, because she refused to let it happen. It was a simple matter of getting a rental car while her Scion spent a few days getting painted. No big. The car wasn't a huge deal. It was Laura's choice of word that fueled Cassidy's anger. For the moment, though, she pushed it all aside and focused on Brynn, hoping like hell Pinky still wanted to have a sleepover.

"I think that's a good idea," Brynn said, keeping her stare on the goings-on outside the car. "I don't think I could explain that to my daddy."

"Yeah, I'm not looking forward to explaining it to my mom, either."

Brynn finally turned her head toward Cassidy. The rims of her eyes were red, as if she'd been sitting there the entire time quietly crying. "Your mom doesn't know already?"

"Nope. She's huge on LGBT rights, though, so I think she'd understand. I just haven't had the chance to talk to her about it since we've had... um, other stuff going on."

"I just assumed you guys talked about everything. You seem like the type."

"We do. Usually."

Cassidy pulled into the driveway, cut the engine, and took a deep breath. Before she had a chance to think of the best way to explain the situation, her mother and grandmother walked out of the house dressed in their gardening best.

Crrrraaaap.

Miranda's eyes widened, and Nana dropped the basket of gardening tools she was carrying. "What in the Sam Hill?" her grandmother cried.

"Who did this?" her mother demanded, storming over to the car with Nana hot on her heels. Cassidy slid from the driver's side and looked over the roof of her car at Brynn, who was standing in her all too familiar "earth swallow me now" pose.

"Laura Dorien did it while Brynn and I were in the mall."

"Why?" her mother urged again.

"Teen girls nowadays are little—" Nana cut herself off, probably for Brynn's sake more than anyone else's.

"She thinks Brynn and I are lesbians 'cause we were holding hands." Maybe Brynn didn't want that particular detail aired, but Cassidy had no shame when it came to her divorced mother and widowed grandmother. The three of them were close, and she briefly wondered why she hadn't sat down earlier with her mom and told her about her sexual orientation.

"Holding hands?" Nana looked like she'd been slapped hard. "Some girl did this because you were *holding hands?*"

"That's preposterous! Girls hold hands all the time," her mother chimed in.

Nana pursed her lips. The look on her face was one Cassidy knew all too well. She'd worn it almost permanently when Cassidy's father had been moving out, and it crossed her features every time Miranda mentioned the man, even in passing conversation.

"Lesbians? Because of a little hand holding? I'll show her a lesbian!"

Cassidy caught Brynn's equally surprised expression from the corner of her eye, just before she focused on her grandmother. "Calm down, Nana. It's whatever. The insurance can cover it, and I'll handle the chick at school."

Apparently, Cassidy's mother wasn't as willing to ignore Nana's previous statement. She glanced over at the elderly woman, one brow quirked in curiosity and a half smile on her face.

"What do you know about lesbians, Mom?"

"I've been in love with a woman before—" Nana turned to Cassidy, offering her a smile. "Before your grandfather, of course. It was a long time ago, but we were happy until her family moved away to England. We did a whole lot more than hold hands too."

"Mom!" Miranda exclaimed as she laughed softly.

Brynn giggled, the sound eliciting a broad smile from Cassidy.

The three women in Cassidy's life were all standing in the sunshine, laughing despite the catastrophe that had just befallen her precious car. It made her realize nothing was really as bad as it seemed, and for a moment, she even contemplated letting Laura get away with what she'd done. That only lasted a moment, though.

When Nana offered to make a batch of her famous white chocolate chip macadamia cookies, Cassidy explained they were going to Brynn's house for a minute but they'd be back to have a sleepover and eat plenty of cookies in a little while.

Her mother walked over, closing the distance between them. The soft smile on her beautiful features made her big blue eyes crinkle at the edges, but it didn't diminish the dynamics of her mesmerizing stare. She lowered her forehead to rest against Cassidy's. "I won't pressure you about it, but you do know that you can talk to me about anything, right?"

"Yes, Mom. I know. And I will. Promise."

"Okay, sweetheart." Miranda pressed her heart-shaped lips to Cassidy's warm cheek in a loving kiss before pulling away and smiling over the roof of the car at Brynn, who still stood on the passenger side.

"Brynn, I'll see you later?"

"Yes, ma'am," Brynn said.

"Call me Miranda, please. Ma'am is for my mother."

Nana snorted. "Not even. You can call me Nana."

For the second time since discovering Laura's handiwork, Brynn smiled. "Okay, Miranda and Nana it is. Um… I guess we'll be back in a little bit?" It was more of a question than a statement, one directed at Cassidy, who took that as her cue to close the car door behind her before walking around and boldly lacing her fingers through Brynn's.

"Yep. Be back in no time."

Nana smiled proudly. "Before cookies, let's get back to those petunias, shall we? They won't prune themselves, you know." With that, Cassidy's still-smiling grandmother took Miranda's arm and led her back to the garden bed and the step where she'd dropped the basket of tools moments before.

Cassidy turned to Brynn. Even though Pinky was still smiling, a hint of worry remained in the depths of her gorgeous gaze. If she could take a stick to Laura's head for every time she had caused that needless worry to blossom, the chick would be a puddle of pulp by now. *That* was what irritated Cassidy the most—no matter how many times she tried to convince Brynn that Laura couldn't do anything, she still let worry over the possibilities cloud her happiness.

Chapter 21

THE moment Brynn's house came into view, she let go of Cassidy's fingers and stuffed both hands down into the tight pockets of the white jeans Cassidy had dressed her in before leaving for the mall. She didn't want her parents to see the two of them holding hands, didn't want them getting any ideas—whether their ideas were wrong or right. No way could Brynn begin to explain the relationship that had formed between her and Cassidy.

She felt Cassidy staring at her, though Brynn didn't want to acknowledge it. It was bad enough she couldn't come clean to her folks, but to have to apologize for being so afraid of everything made the situation ten times worse.

"We'll just tell them I'm spending the night at your house so we can work on our project," Brynn offered, keeping her nervous stare trained on the house.

"Whatever you wanna do."

"It's not exactly what I *want* to do. It's kinda what I *need* to do right now."

"I understand."

And she was so glad Cassidy did understand. Most people would've been completely put off by having to sneak around and hide, but apparently, Cassidy wasn't most people—a point she continued to make every time they hung out.

Brynn opened the front door, and she immediately heard her little sister's video game screeching through the otherwise peaceful house. They rounded the corner into the living room and were met with the seizure-inducing strobing lights bouncing off the TV.

"Where's Mom and Dad?" Brynn asked.

Her little sister didn't even raise her head. "Mom's outside, and I think Daddy is in his office."

"Thanks."

Nothing. Not so much as a "You're welcome." Brynn rolled her eyes, then nodded, signaling for Cassidy to follow her to the backyard. They found Brynn's mom kneeling down in the grass on the edge of one of her many flowerbeds, tilling or digging or whatever people did when they worked in the garden.

"Mom?" Brynn said softly.

Her mother raised her head, strawberry blonde curls framing her rosy, freckled face. The sweat on her forehead glistened in the afternoon sun. She stood from the foamy pad she'd been kneeling on and pulled off her gloves, smiling as she looked the two of them over.

"That's a cute outfit. Where did you get it from?" her mother asked.

"It belongs to Cassidy." Brynn thumbed over her shoulder to Cassidy, who'd been quietly standing behind her. "This is Cassidy Rivers, Mom."

Both Brynn's mother and Brynn's new gal pal/girlfriend-type-person took a step forward, offering their hands. Brynn's mother smiled and said, "Nice to finally meet you, Cassidy."

"The pleasure is all mine, Mrs. Michaels," Cassidy replied with a polite smile.

"So, Mom," Brynn said. Her mother released Cassidy's hand. "I'm gonna spend the night with Cassidy, if that's cool. We have that project thingy still, and we both want to get a jump on everyone else. Is that okay?"

"Did you ask your father?"

"No, ma'am. I didn't see him."

"Well, I'm sure it won't be a problem." Brynn's mom looked over at Cassidy and asked, "You live just around the corner, right?"

"Yes, ma'am." Cassidy nodded, pointing in the direction of her home. "At 6830 Briarwood Lane. At the end of the block and around the corner."

"Well, I suppose it's okay, as long as Cassidy's mother doesn't mind. Just leave the home phone number on the whiteboard on the fridge, okay?"

"Yes, ma'am," Brynn responded dutifully.

"It was nice to meet you, Cassidy," her mother said.

"Likewise, Mrs. Michaels."

"You girls have fun."

"We will," Brynn said as she grabbed Cassidy's wrist and quickly dragged her back into the house before her mother had a chance to ask any more questions or make any more demands.

They stopped at the fridge, and Brynn handed Cassidy the dry-erase marker so she could write down the number, then they headed upstairs and into Brynn's bedroom.

It was the first time Cassidy had ever been in her room, and Brynn was so anxious to grab her things and haul out of there, she hadn't stopped to consider what Cassidy might think of the dark, emo design of the cave where Brynn often hid away from the world. Brynn chewed her bottom lip as she looked over the black and purple decor. Surely, Cassidy had plenty of little quips just begging to spill from her lips. God, if Cassidy started cracking jokes….

"Let me just grab something to sleep in and my laptop, then we can go back to your house," Brynn said.

Cassidy walked over to the big beanbag and plopped down, seemingly comfortable with her surroundings. Her gaze shifted from one end of the room to the other. She looked like she was taking in every last little detail in order to better arm herself with commentary. When she looked back at Brynn, there was a hint of a smile tugging the edges of her lips upward.

"You know, this isn't what I expected at all," Cassidy finally said. "I was thinking there'd be sparkling vampires and skulls everywhere. This is... serene. I like it in here." She leaned over and picked up one of the books at the base of the purple beanbag.

Brynn frowned. She waited for the punch line, waited for a snippy joke, but Cassidy only sat there thumbing through the book she'd picked up. Brynn opened her mouth, closed it, and then opened it again. "No jokes?"

"Jokes about what?"

"About my Batcave room...."

"Um... do you want me to joke? I already pointed out the lack of sparkly fangers."

"No. No jokes, please." Brynn went back to digging in her dresser for some pajamas. "I'm already freaked out about you seeing my room."

The book landed on the floor with a soft thud. Brynn heard it but didn't turn around. She assumed Cassidy was off to do a little more exploring, which honestly scared the hell out of her. Not that she had anything to truly be embarrassed about. She just didn't want Cassidy Rivers thinking her any stranger than she already did. But then she felt Cassidy's arms wrap around her waist and felt Cassidy's chin on her shoulder. She smelled the floral perfume and the strawberry scent of her lips, and the breath caught in Brynn's throat.

"Why are you so freaked about me seeing your room?" Cassidy whispered. "It's nice. There's touches of feminism, and there aren't any bloody, headless bats anywhere. Chill, yeah?"

Brynn stopped worrying with her bottom lip long enough to smile, even though Cassidy probably couldn't see it. The sincerity in Cassidy's words and the softness of her voice was enough to make anyone "chill." It made Brynn relax in her arms.

"I can totally chill," she said a little airily. "Totally."

"Totally, huh?" A soft snicker left Cassidy before she unwrapped her arms from Brynn, then squeezed between her and the dresser. "You're totally starting to sound like me."

Heat exploded in Brynn's cheeks. She knew right then just how bad she was crushing on Cassidy Rivers. Before, it had been a faint feeling, like wishing for chocolate, but not really craving it. Oh no, now, she knew just how badly she *craved* Cassidy.

Brynn licked her suddenly dry lips, lowered her eyes, and stammered through a bunch of "uhs" and "ums" before finally saying, "I don't know how to respond to that."

"Don't worry 'bout it. The blush on your cheeks is speaking for you. Finished?"

"Yeah, I, um… I think I am."

"Well then, let's go. Nana's cookies are waiting for us," Cassidy said in her usual take-charge tone.

She took a step back, giving Brynn enough space to zip up her bag and sling it over one shoulder. Brynn barely had enough time to look around for something she might be missing. Cassidy's fingers wrapped around her wrist, and she tugged her out of the room, down the stairs, and outside into the warm, California sunshine.

Clearly, Cassidy was pretty excited about her grandmother's cookies. Brynn had never seen her walk so briskly for anything. She usually just paced along, taking an interest in her surroundings. This time, she could have broken a land speed record for how quickly she made it back to her house.

At the front porch, Cassidy turned to Brynn, beaming brightly. "I'm so excited for you to sleep over! I can't wait!"

Whoa. Maybe it wasn't the cookies that had Cassidy in such a hurry after all.

Chapter 22

"MOM? Nana? We're back," Cassidy called out, still holding onto Brynn's wrist as she led her through the contemporary home.

Her grandmother called out from the kitchen in a soft, singsong tone. "Those petunias were a bit—well, they were damn difficult. I just now started on the dough, so you girls can go get ready for your sleepover or do whatever it is that girls do nowadays to hang out." She put emphasis on the "hang out" part of her statement, almost as if the older woman was silently implicating something else.

God, her family rocked.

"Okay, we'll be in my room," Cassidy replied before continuing to tug Brynn along like a rag doll, all the way up the stairs, past the second floor landing, and straight into her bedroom. Only when the door shut behind them did she seem to finally take a breath and relax.

"Um… well, jeez. Now what?" she asked with a little giggle.

Brynn crossed the room and set her bag down on the floor next to Cassidy's dresser. Her little Pinky looked so at home there now, almost as at home as she appeared in her own room. "We could…. I don't know. Watching a movie seems so lame." Brynn shook her head. "So does working on our project."

"No, none of that stuff."

Cassidy had been thinking about her mother's words from a few nights before. The way her anger sparked her magic earlier at the mall with Laura really made those words sink in. It was apparently time to start coming to terms with the gift she'd inherited. There was really no way to do that without telling Brynn about it, since she truly wanted Brynn involved in every aspect of her life. Besides that, she didn't want to hide anything from her.

"I have a better idea, but you have to trust me, and you have to promise not to freak out. Can you do that?" she asked, as she walked to where Brynn stood, staring cautiously at her from behind the part in her light pink bangs.

"You're asking *me* to trust *you*." Brynn frowned, thumbing at her own chest.

"Yes. I am. With something very, very important."

"Cassidy, we kissed. You've seen me mostly naked. I think it's safe to say I trust you."

Well, she had a point there. Still, Cassidy needed to hear Brynn say those words. Three little, not so big of a deal words, but for some reason, it meant so much to her. Maybe it was because for the longest time, she didn't think Brynn would ever really come to trust her at all, let alone even a little bit. Now, standing in front of her, she felt like the last of her secrets were about to be spilled. The very last thing she kept hidden away from the whole world, save for her family, was about to become something else she could share with Brynn. There really were no words to explain how that made Cassidy feel.

"Okay… I don't really know how to tell you this, so I'm just gonna show you. But remember you said you wouldn't freak out, 'kay?"

One step. Two steps. Three steps back. When she was far away enough from Brynn that she couldn't hurt or startle her, Cassidy nodded toward the book on her nightstand. Brynn's piercing gaze shifted to the Dickens tome. She stood frozen in place with something in between confusion and intrigue gracing her features.

Swiping her suddenly sweaty palms across the front of her T-shirt, Cassidy took one last, steadying breath before raising a hand, palm up, toward the book. The paperback began to gently shake. It started off as a barely visible tremble, really. Within seconds, however, it raised into the air, hovering just above the whitewashed wood of the table it had sat on. Slowly, Cassidy made a "come hither" motion with her hand, urging the book to float across the room until it rested in the open palm of her hand.

When she looked back over at Brynn, her eyes were wide as golf balls and her mouth was agape. Uh-oh.

"Please don't freak out. I can't help it. I was born this way. So was my mom and my grandmother and a whole line of women before us, dating back to before the eighteen hundreds."

Cassidy's mouth suddenly went dry. She continued to stammer excuses at the still-silent Brynn, in hopes she could stop her from doing what she looked like she was going to do—bolt from the room.

"It's not evil or anything. I'm not bad, I swear. I… I just… it's magic, but it's not bad. I can't cause harm to people or anything like that. I can only use it for good, because whatever I do comes three times back to me. Please, please don't leave me," Cassidy implored one last time, not really caring about how desperate she sounded at the moment.

"That. That. That." Jesus, she'd fried Brynn's brain. So. Not. Good. "Was that—" Brynn swallowed so hard Cassidy saw the waving of her throat. "—real magic?"

"Um, yeah. About as real as it gets. No potions or spells or chanting over voodoo dolls with pins inside. Just… magical power."

"You're a… a… a real witch? Like, really real?"

"Well, you won't see any pointy hats in my closet, if that's what you're expecting," Cassidy said, setting the book down on the bed beside her so she could reach out and gently take Brynn's hands in hers. "But yeah. We're real witches. Are you scared?"

"Not scared," Brynn said, tightening her fingers around Cassidy's hands. "I'm, um… surprised. I've read about witches, but I didn't think they were real… like, *really* real. I mean, I know they're real, but not like that." She exhaled sharply, as if she'd been hanging onto that breath for a while. "I've heard of Wiccans and even read a bunch about it, but somehow, I think this is different. Isn't it?"

"Yes and no. I mean, kinda. Wiccans are Pagans, and we're Pagan, but we're not Wiccan. It's kind of like saying Christianity and Catholicism. Like, all Catholics are Christians but not all Christians are Catholics." Cassidy blinked, hoping that made sense to Brynn, who thankfully was still standing in the room and hadn't run for the tree lines of Majestic Hills.

"Brynn, please. Please, you can't tell anyone about this, 'kay? For *so* many reasons, but mainly for my family's safety. Please…." Cassidy's voice had a vulnerable urgency to it. She could hear it in her tone, but she needed Brynn to know exactly how much was at stake if she spoke a word of what she'd seen to anyone.

"I wouldn't do that to you," Brynn whispered. "I wouldn't want anything bad to happen to you."

Much like before with her trust, Cassidy had needed to hear Brynn say she would keep her secret. That she wouldn't tell anyone. Once she had, the breath Cassidy had been holding in came blowing out past her glossy lips.

"Thank you," she said. For some reason, however, she kept talking. "It's just that I've never told anyone about that before, and I'm kinda scared, ya know? I mean, the entire world is full of people like me, but we're hidden. We keep that part of ourselves to family and only really, really close people like husbands, kids, etcetera—"

Her words were abruptly cut off by a mouth pressing against hers. Her eyes widened. Never once did she expect Brynn to be the one to initiate a kiss, but as she lived and breathed, her Pinky had her in a lip-lock of unbreakable proportions.

That Witch!

THE anxiety and freak-out vibe coming off Cassidy was enough to knock Brynn off her feet, and the only thing Brynn could think of to make her "chill"—like Cassidy kept asking her to do—was plant her lips over Cassidy's. It was a bold move, one Brynn didn't really see herself ever being able to take, but there they were, kissing… again.

There was something very different about the kiss this time. It felt easier, more natural. It felt like the right thing to do. Maybe because Brynn had finally admitted to herself that she craved Cassidy in a way she'd never craved anyone else before. Maybe Brynn was starting to come to terms with how she felt and what she liked. She wasn't sure, but she did know that her lips belonged to Cassidy. Explicitly.

She lifted away from Cassidy's lips and gave her a hooded smile. "I, um… sorry," she said breathlessly.

When Cassidy's lids opened again, her smile reflected in the crinkles at the edges of her eyes, making her gaze sparkle. "Sorry? Don't be sorry. I like the way you shut me up."

"I didn't mean it like that. It's just, you were worrying and freaking out and—"

Cassidy pressed her palm to Brynn's mouth and gave her that beautiful pink smile Brynn had become a complete sucker for. Brynn had the urge to kiss those delicious lips again, but Nana calling "The cookies are hot—come and get 'em" from the bottom of the stairs stopped her.

Chapter 23

BETWEEN the four women, the dozen and a half cookies were gone without so much as a crumb left behind. When the festivities were over and Nana said she was done for the night, Cassidy's mother decided to dismiss herself too. She said she wanted to get a little reading done before bed. As far as Brynn was concerned, the fewer people nosing around the house the better. Maybe she could convince Cassidy to show her more magic. Then maybe they could kiss again, or even better, they could snuggle in the bed.

The idea of being that close to Cassidy made Brynn feel all warm inside. And ironically, none of those feelings really scared Brynn anymore, well, not as much as they had before.

Well, the feelings didn't scare her, but the possible repercussions of being true to herself sure did. Every time she thought about her parents catching her or someone at school finding out she had a thing for Cassidy Rivers, her stomach knotted to the point of being painful.

They returned to Cassidy's room, and Brynn flopped down across Cassidy's bed. Her body felt twenty pounds heavier than it had been before she'd eaten all those cookies. She laid her hand across her bloated belly and said, "Those were delicious and all, but *oh my God*, I'm miserable."

"I'm used to cookies for dinner. It happens at least once whenever Nana comes to town for a visit. My mom's liberal that way," Cassidy said casually as she sank down beside Brynn, sprawling out across her queen-size bed.

"Lucky. We're a 'better eat all your veggies' household. I didn't even know the glory of chocolate until I was in junior high school."

Cassidy's cobalt eyes widened. "What? How's that even humanly possible? What about Halloween candy? Did you get to eat that?" Cassidy looked like she was trying to understand quantum physics.

"We never celebrated Halloween. Daddy didn't let us. When we were kids, we did things at the church. I stopped going when I grew out of it. My little sister does from time to time, though."

"Lovely. Your parents are hardcore religious and conservative and your girlfriend's a lesbian witch. You're gonna have fun explaining *that* one."

"Girlfriend?" Brynn turned her head toward Cassidy. Was it official? Were they...? "Am I your girlfriend?"

"Um, I meant...." Cassidy looked away suddenly, but Brynn caught a glimpse of the crimson flooding her cheeks. "I... er... we... um... I guess? I mean, are you?"

Brynn smiled and moved closer to Cassidy. She felt so completely silly for doing it, but she reached down and ran her fingers over Cassidy's knuckles. "I think I would like to be," she whispered. "If that's okay with you."

"Uh, yeaaaaah. It's... I.... Yeah. I want that...."

"Then I guess I'm your girlfriend now." A teasing smile curled one corner of Brynn's lips. "Does that mean you'll show me more magic?"

At the mention of more magic, Cassidy looked like she could have, for a moment, been knocked off the edge of the bed. "More magic? You really wanna see more stuff?" The hope and happiness in her voice couldn't be measured or put into words.

"Yeah, I do. It's kinda cool, ya know?"

"It kinda is, yeah. Um... okay." Cassidy sat up, looking around her room. She pointed to a light pink candle sitting on her desk. "Watch that candle, 'kay?"

Brynn nodded excitedly as she sat up on the bed and tucked her legs under her body, sitting lotus style like she'd learned in those stupid yoga classes her mom had dragged her to. She bit down on her bottom lip to contain the wide goofy smile on her face and set her stare on the candle like Cassidy asked.

The sound of Cassidy's fingers snapping together almost made her look away, but before she could, the candle sparked to life. The wick lit up, blazing brightly before dimming down to a light flicker. She thought she heard Cassidy whisper something in a language she couldn't decipher, but she was too enthralled by the flame to ask.

"Wait for it," Cassidy said.

"There's more?"

"Uh-huh."

Just then, the flame's glow began to change colors—dimming from orange to a light yellow before changing to a soft blue hue. The colors cycled through the shades of the rainbow before finally ending up a light purple.

"Oh my God! Cassidy, that's the coolest thing I've ever seen," Brynn declared. "What other stuff can you do? Can you fly? Oh my God, can you ride a broom?"

"Yes. I also really do have that pointy hat I told you I didn't own, and we keep a cauldron in the yard."

The sarcasm in Cassidy's voice wasn't lost on Brynn at all. "Ha ha," she said as she gave Cassidy a playful shove. "My girlfriend's a smartass."

Girlfriend. It was getting so easy to call Cassidy that one little word with such huge meaning.

"Well, smartass is better than dumbass, right?"

"Touché," Brynn said with a giggle.

They spent the rest of the night talking and laughing and stealing the occasional kiss from each other. Cassidy shared more of her magic, and Brynn anxiously watched, hanging on every moment as it passed. Brynn couldn't get enough of everything that was Cassidy.

When the evening wound down and they were both too tired to keep their eyes open any longer, they decided to change into their pajamas, and this time, Brynn didn't hesitate changing in front of Cassidy. And when Cassidy lifted away her top and changed into a thin, light blue camisole, Brynn couldn't tear her eyes away. *Her* cheerleader had the most beautiful body, so beautiful Brynn wanted to feel Cassidy's soft skin against the palms of her hands, but she fought her urges. She let her eyes enjoy what her hands would have to wait for.

They climbed beneath the covers of Cassidy's queen-size bed, and though there was plenty of space for them to have their own sides, they met in the middle—bodies pressed together, arms around each other, the tips of their noses gently touching. Brynn smiled softly as she stared into Cassidy's incredible blue eyes.

Chapter 24

SUNDAY passed by slow as molasses for Cassidy. After Nana made blueberry pancakes for breakfast and the girls had hearty stacks piled high and dripping with organic maple syrup, Brynn went home so Cassidy could focus on what her mother and grandmother wanted to teach her. Sure enough, Cassidy almost backed out of the lesson again, but Brynn convinced her to go through with it. So of course, like a lovesick puppy, she obeyed without further complaint.

The day moved along with Nana teaching Cassidy how to better channel her emotions into her powers as opposed to her emotions controlling the magic running through her. By the end of the day, Cassidy had gained a new harness over her abilities. She practiced a little spell work too, as well as started her very own book of shadows, which Nana gave her. It was a beautiful book with a pentacle burned into the aged leather cover. Inside were thick parchment pages and a dedication from Nana scribbled on the first page that read:

For my dearest Cassidy,

May the elements of the earth combine with the power running through you to create magic the likes of which this world has never seen. You are bound for greatness. Don't forget where you come from.

Love, Nana.

Cassidy had gone to sleep anticipating Monday, when she could tell Brynn all about the new things she'd learned. Since her mother had to take the Scion to the body shop before picking up a rental car, Brynn offered to give Cassidy a ride to school.

Now Cassidy stood in front of the mirror, looking over the outfit she'd chosen. She'd done her hair in soft waves that cascaded over a sleeveless, light yellow Michael Kors tunic. Her dark blue Citizens of Humanity skinny jeans hugged her athletic legs and ended tightly at the ankles to accent her Stella McCartney ballet flats. Admittedly, she'd been toning down her usually preppy attire since she started hanging out with Brynn, but there was only so much in her closet that didn't scream "Cassidy Rivers, label whore."

As she contemplated taking Brynn on a shopping spree so they could both get some new threads, a car horn beeped twice outside. Cassidy swiped her phone from the desk and grabbed her backpack before tearing down the stairs and out the front door, calling out "I'm going to school, Mom!" over her shoulder. She closed the door and bounded down the driveway to Brynn's car, where her girlfriend sat, still a little sleepy-eyed but smiling brightly.

God, that smile is something to look forward to in the mornings.

After settling down into the passenger side, she leaned over and pressed a chaste kiss to Brynn's cheek. Cassidy tossed her backpack into the backseat and buckled her seat belt, and they were on their way, weaving through the streets of Majestic Hills.

They talked about their Sunday away from each other. While they'd been texting throughout the day, Cassidy was learning magic, and Brynn attended a church picnic with her family, so there were details each girl had to share. Brynn told Cassidy of the fun she'd actually had talking to a few kids who were also in attendance with their families. She recounted every minute detail. The tasty macaroni salad she'd had two servings of. The way her little sister was reprimanded for throwing fruit punch on a boy who called her "snotface." Brynn's father's inclination to embarrass her when the pastor asked if Brynn would like to attend one of the church's free abstinence seminars for teens by replying, "She's going to be abstinent until she marries the future president of the United States."

Cassidy laughed the entire ride, and all too soon they were pulling into the parking lot of Majestic Hills High, faced with another long week of hiding the way they felt about each other. More days of sneaking glances and concealing moments of closeness behind the guise of schoolwork. Brynn clearly felt the same, because the minute she cut off the engine, she turned to Cassidy with her bottom lip tucked between her teeth.

"If last week was tough, this week's gonna be even harder now that we're, um… dating."

"Yeah, I was just thinking about that."

"Well, maybe we could find a youth group." Brynn unclicked her seat belt and reached back for her black backpack. "You know, just so we can be ourselves somewhere."

"I really like that idea. I have cheer practice every Monday, Wednesday, and Friday, but maybe we can figure something out around that schedule."

Brynn shot Cassidy a look she probably kept hidden away for really giddy moments. Cassidy thought those precious moments must be few and far between for an emo chick, so this little rarity was priceless to her. Brynn's smile was radiant. It lit up her face, making her eyes sparkle behind the pink fringe of her bangs.

"I'd like that," she said softly.

"Well, then that's what we'll do, Brynnie. Let's get to class, yeah?"

Cassidy was itching to lean over and kiss those smiling lips. Since they were parked in the school lot with kids ambling past Brynn's car, all she could do was grab her backpack and wink at Brynn before popping up from the car. She got as far as closing the door and hiking her bag up her shoulder when she heard Laura's annoyingly grating voice from somewhere in the near distance.

"Aww, where's your car, Cassidy?"

Brynn's pink head shot up from the driver's side. Beneath her bangs, Cassidy could see her wide eyes and nervous expression. Cassidy merely winked at her before turning to look at Laura, who stood by the little Honda Civic donning a smug look.

"Oh, hey, Laura," Cassidy replied with her own smug expression. "You know, since Brynn and I are so close now... like, I'm practically her BFF, we've decided to start sharing rides to school. Don't be jelly."

Laura was good at maintaining composure, but Cassidy had it on lock. The emo wannabe's face glowed with anger, crimson lighting up her cheeks as her hands white-knuckled the folder she was clutching to her chest. Cassidy gave her her best saccharin-induced smile and wiggled her fingers in a wave before walking around to Brynn's side.

"Do you think that was a good idea?" Brynn asked while peering in Laura's direction.

"Meh." Cassidy shrugged. "I already told you I've got this. There's a few things set in place for her should she decide to mess with you."

"Yeah, but what about you? You saw what she did to your car."

"That was cannon fodder."

"I hope you know what you're doing," Brynn said, seemingly not convinced. "The bell's about to ring. I'll see you later, right?"

"Yep. Mrs. Miller's class. It's a date—" Cassidy's words were cut off by Laura, who all but plowed into her on her way toward the school building.

Really? Is that all she's got?

Laura would have to try harder. Cassidy was a cheerleader, after all, and wasn't easily knocked off her feet. Laura, on the other hand, probably wasn't blessed with such balance. Yeah, her magic should only be used for good, but Cassidy opted to abandon that belief just once and made Laura trip over her own two feet.

It was worth whatever consequence she'd have to pay.

Laura's notebook flew from her hands as she tumbled forward to meet the asphalt face-first, and that's when Cassidy really struck. She walked over to where Laura was, pressed one Stella McCartney ballet flat over her hand, and grinned down at her as she said, "They say cows tip over easily. I'd watch my step if I were you."

The laughter ringing out around them fueled Cassidy's need to keep the battle going. Unfortunately, Laura stumbled onto her feet, swiped her notebook from the ground, and shuffled the fallen papers inside. Without a word or even a glance in Cassidy's direction, she humbly walked away, leaving Cassidy a little disappointed they didn't get to fight it out. Surely there'd be other chances, though. By the end of the school week, Laura would be the laughingstock of Majestic Hills High.

If only Brynn were okay with Cassidy's plans, she'd be more comfortable with it all. Pinky still had that conscience thing going on. She never said anything, but that was just the type of person Brynn was. Caring and compassionate, especially toward people who meant something to her. Laura definitely meant something to Brynn, even if the level of that "something" had diminished with each and every bullying antic Laura pulled.

As Cassidy headed toward the building, the only issue nagging at her was who was more important to Brynn, her or Laura?

Chapter 25

THE school day passed, and Cassidy and Laura stayed on Brynn's mind—through math and science, lunch, and PE. Brynn didn't stop thinking about what had gone down before school. She worried Cassidy would do something truly cruel and Laura would become a laughingstock. Laura probably deserved as much, in all honesty, but Brynn didn't want the girl she cared about being the one dishing out Laura's punishment. Couldn't they just leave that up to karma?

Brynn took her regular spot in Mrs. Miller's class and opened the book she and Cassidy had chosen for the next part of their project. She quietly read along, minding her own business until she heard Cassidy say, "Get out of my way."

The sound of her girlfriend's voice made Brynn raise her head.

Cassidy was glaring at Laura, and Laura glowered right back at her. Brynn couldn't believe Laura wasn't backing down. Whatever happened to that whole "staying off Cassidy's radar" thing, and why did Laura insist on causing problems now?

Oh, the answer was as clear as day when Cassidy took the spot where Laura normally sat—right beside Brynn, and Brynn couldn't bring herself to look either girl in the eyes. Something would have to give. Laura needed to stop pushing Cassidy's buttons, and Cassidy, well… she kinda needed to do the same. If things kept going this way, Brynn had a feeling it would turn out disastrous.

"Brynnie," Cassidy said. Her voice immediately got Brynn's attention, even as she heard Laura huffing angrily from somewhere behind them. "I have cheer practice after school. You don't have to wait around for me if you have stuff to do."

"I know," Brynn whispered. "I don't mind waiting for you."

"Okies then."

Brynn gave her a soft smile. She was about to say something else when Mrs. Miller called the class to attention. Their teacher began reading an excerpt from one of Brynn's favorite Sylvia Plath books— *The Bell Jar*. In her soft, weathered voice she read, "The silence depressed me. It wasn't the silence of silence. It was my own silence."

For reasons Brynn truly understood, that passage nailed her right in the gut. Her silence, in regards to her true being and her feelings for Cassidy, depressed her. It was her own silence, forced upon her by her fear. Didn't they both deserve better?

The longer class dragged on, the more Brynn became lost in her thoughts. Part of her wished she could hold Cassidy's hand in front of the entire school and kiss her no matter who was watching. Part of her wished she could stand up to everyone and admit how deep her feelings for Cassidy were. Then there was her completely coward side that wouldn't let her own how she felt and flip the bird to anyone who didn't like it.

The bell rang, and Brynn didn't even notice. She'd been so lost in thought that the normally nerve-racking, eardrum-shattering sound didn't even bother her. In fact, it took Cassidy reaching across the aisle and giving the sleeve of her hoodie a tug before Brynn snapped out of her daydream.

"Earth to Brynnie. Come in, Brynnie," Cassidy said in a singsong voice.

"Huh? What?" Brynn looked around the room. People were already clearing out. "I was, um… uh… daydreaming, I guess."

A wicked grin crept up on Cassidy's face. "Was it naughty?"

The moment Brynn opened her mouth to answer Cassidy's question, Laura stormed by them so fast it knocked the book off

Brynn's desk. Her best friend—or maybe it was "former" best friend now—glared back at her before disappearing from the classroom. Sighing, Brynn reached down and grabbed her book.

"No. Sorry to disappoint, but it wasn't naughty," Brynn finally said.

"Are you okay? You look… sad," Cassidy asked, all joking gone from her voice as she packed her bag and rose from her seat.

"Not sad. I'm actually pretty happy, all things considered. I guess I'm just… disappointed. Does that make sense?"

"Did I do something to disappoint you?"

"Oh no. No." Brynn stood from her desk and gathered her things. She hefted her backpack up on her shoulders and waited for Cassidy to join her at the end of the row of desks. "I'm disappointed with Laura for being so rancid. And I'm disappointed with myself for not standing up to everyone. It sucks."

"You can always change that, you know. All it takes is a little strength. I know you've got it, just look deep inside for it." Cassidy locked stares with Brynn

"I'm not strong enough, Cassidy. I'm really not."

"We don't really know how strong we are until being strong is the only option left."

"And right now, I have the option of keeping my mouth shut." Brynn glanced around the classroom and noticed everyone was gone, probably halfway to their cars by now. She leaned in and gave Cassidy a chaste kiss on the cheek. "Be careful at practice. I'll be waiting for you by my car."

"Okies. Just, um… just know that you can talk to me 'bout anything, 'kay?"

"I know. You're the only one I *can* talk to."

"That's 'cause you loooooove me… you wanna kisssssss meeee…," Cassidy sang.

Brynn laughed and gave her girlfriend a playful shove. "God, go. You're going to be late."

She laughed as Cassidy bounced out the door, long blonde curls springing with each peppy step. To Brynn's world of darkness, Cassidy Rivers was a welcome ray of sunlight.

Brynn headed in the opposite direction, bypassing her locker. She planned on going to the library to read while she waited on Cassidy to finish practice, but the idea of watching Cassidy's beautiful body move as she performed sounded so much more fun. Brynn could hide beside the bleachers, and no one would ever be the wiser.

The sun outside the school was bright, so bright it blinded Brynn for a second. She flattened her hand to her brow, and the moment her eyes adjusted to the shade, she saw a darkened figure leaning against her car. She took a few steps closer. The figure started to come into focus. Purple hair. Black clothes. Black backpack.

"Laura," she sighed.

Before Brynn had a chance to run and hide, Laura turned her head, and their stares locked. There was absolutely no avoiding the girl now, no avoiding the conversation she'd been waiting to have with her friend.

Laura stood from the side of the car, and she met Brynn halfway across the parking lot. She didn't look happy at all. In fact, she looked downright pissed. Her nostrils flared, and her lips were pursed. Pure anger filled her eyes.

"What are you doing?" Laura asked, tone demanding.

"I'm going to my car," Brynn responded flatly before continuing across the half-empty lot.

"You know what I mean," Laura yelled back. "What are you doing with Cassidy Rivers?"

"Thought you had us all figured out."

"So you're a lesbian now?"

That stopped Brynn dead in her tracks. Her heart sank down into her toes, and her breath hitched. She didn't turn around, fearing the expression on her face might give her away, but didn't her lack of response already give her away?

"What do you care?" she finally asked.

"It's true, isn't it?"

We don't really know how strong we are until being strong is the only option left, she heard the ghost of Cassidy's voice in her head. But did Brynn have the kind of strength it took to admit what she was to someone other than herself and her girlfriend?

She spun around on her booted feet and faced Laura, then took two steps toward her. "Why do you care what I am? What does it matter? Aren't I the same person you became friends with?"

"No. No, you're not. You've changed, and you're always with her. You never want to hang out with me anymore. We never talk or anything!"

"So you're jealous? Is that what this is all about?"

"No. I. Freaking. Hate. Her."

"Why?"

"You're kidding, right?"

"Do I look like I'm kidding?"

"You know what?" Laura said as she tightened her fists around the straps of her backpack. "You can have your fun with her. I'm done. You want to be friends with cheerleaders, have at it. I don't need you."

Before Brynn had a chance to even try rationalizing with Laura, her friend stormed away, heading across the parking lot and over to her own car. She climbed inside, revved the engine, and squealed tires out of the school's lot and down the street.

Honestly, Brynn felt horrible for the way things went down with Laura. She didn't mean for the conversation to go the way it did. She didn't mean to treat Laura that way, but everything spun out of control before Brynn could get a handle on the situation. Now Laura hated her.

She climbed up on the hood of her car, popped her earbuds in, and pulled the book she'd been reading out of her backpack. Everything would be okay as soon as Cassidy finished practice. They could go back to Cassidy's house and work on their project just like they'd planned, and forget everything that had happened with Laura.

Chapter 26

CASSIDY sat drenched in sweat in the passenger seat of Brynn's car. The air conditioning vents were pointed at her, but she was still hella hot. Not that it mattered. From the moment she'd finished practice and found Brynn at her car in the desolate parking lot, she'd known something was wrong with her girlfriend. She thought about asking, but Brynn had looked so happy to see her, she decided to let Pinky open up on her own instead.

Ten minutes into their ride, Brynn still hadn't uttered a word about what had her so upset. Cassidy finally broke down and turned in her seat to face Brynn's profile.

"Okay, what's wrong? And don't say 'nothing', 'cause I can tell it's something."

"Laura met me at my car today. She's so mad at me. I, um… don't think we're friends anymore," Brynn admitted.

That should've made Cassidy happy, but it didn't. Actually, she felt really crappy about it. Not because she disliked Laura, but because she knew how much Brynn cared about her, and losing someone you care about was always hard.

"I'm sorry," she offered quietly. "I know how close you two were. Is there anything you can do to fix it?"

"Short of turning my back on you, no."

"You know you can do that if it means saving your friendship. I'd understand."

"That's not going to happen," Brynn said without a moment of hesitation, as if she didn't even need a second to consider the possibility. "I don't want to be without you, and if Laura can't be happy for me, then I guess she wasn't the friend I thought she was."

Cassidy Rivers, welcome to a rock and a hard place.

Seriously, what was she supposed to do here? On one hand, she wanted Brynn to have friendships she felt comfortable with and wanted her to be happy. On the other hand, she didn't want to lose Brynn because of it. As she sat and thought about how to reply to Brynn without sounding like a needy witch or an arrogant ass, Brynn groaned and said, "Now what?"

When Cassidy looked up, she saw Laura's Honda Civic parked in the driveway to the Michaelses' home. "Oh for frick's sake!"

"Why would she be here? Why?" Brynn's voice grew louder and louder. "Didn't she say all she needed to already? What could she possibly want with me?"

"Chillax, Brynnie. Maybe she's here to apologize for being such a psycho."

Yeah, maybe, but it was highly unlikely. Cassidy had the distinct feeling that something horrible was about to happen. Call it her spidey senses, but her gut tingled in the way people describe butterflies in their stomach—only instead of butterflies, they were zombies. Really mean, hungry ones at that. "Or maybe she wants to get her stuff? Surely there's got to be some of her things in your room, right?"

"Who knows?" Brynn said flatly as she pulled up next to Laura's Honda. She parked and sat there for a long moment, staring up at the house with absolute dread. "We won't find out if we just sit here."

"You want me to come in with you? I promise I'll behave, regardless of what she says or does to me." It was a huge promise, but Cassidy would try her hardest not to make the situation any more difficult than it already was for Brynn, who looked like someone had killed her bunny rabbit.

"Please," Brynn said as she turned the key and shut her car off. She grabbed her backpack out of the backseat and met Cassidy at the concrete walkway. They headed up to the front door together. A unified front, indivisible and unwavering.

As soon as Brynn turned the handle of the door, those zombies in Cassidy's tummy began a full-on assault. Her hands began to quiver slightly, and a feeling of dread sparked through every cell in her body. It was only made worse when she heard Laura's voice coming from the living room to her left, and Mr. Michaels's stern voice calling out, "Brynn, is that you? I need to speak with you, young lady."

Zombies? You've officially killed Cassidy Rivers.

BRYNN felt all the blood rush from her face. Her heart thumped hard inside her chest. She knew that voice. That was her father's concerned voice, colored with a hint of anger. Whatever Laura had done, there was no going back from. Brynn would never forgive her.

She gave Cassidy one last look, then stepped through the living room doorway. Her daddy sat in his recliner and her mom at the edge of the sofa closest to him. Laura sat on the end, smirking as Brynn made her appearance. Thank God she had Cassidy behind her. With Cassidy there, she knew she could maintain a certain level of control just to keep from embarrassing herself in front of her girlfriend.

"Yes, Daddy?" Brynn asked, hesitation coloring her shaky voice.

"Have a seat." He nodded toward the chair on the other side of the room. Cassidy didn't immediately follow her. Instead, she stood by the door. That is, until Brynn's dad said, "You might as well come in and have a seat. Apparently, this involves you too."

Cassidy looked about as nervous as a long-tailed cat in a room full of rocking chairs. She wrung her hands as she silently made her way into the room. She took a seat between Laura and Brynn's mother. "Yes, sir" was all she managed, but she kept her chin up and didn't avert her eyes. Cassidy wasn't ashamed.

"Is there something you need to tell us, Brynn?" her father asked.

He kept his expression stoic, and Brynn felt completely lost. She looked over at her mom for some hint as to how she was supposed to answer that question and came up blank. Her mom only sat there staring down at her fidgeting fingers. Of course, Laura gave nothing away either... other than looking pleased with herself.

"I don't know, Daddy. What is this about?"

He inhaled sharply, sat back in his chair, and crossed his arms over his chest. He didn't take his steely stare off Brynn, and that icy gaze of his only made her heart pound harder.

"Tell me about your 'relationship' with your new friend," he finally said, giving a slight nod toward Cassidy.

No. No. No. This can't be happening to me. How could Laura do this to me?

Brynn's entire body started to shake. Her throat fisted around every short breath she tried to take. She took up the same fidgeting routine her mother had been pulling since the two of them walked into the house. How was she supposed to respond to that? She couldn't very well tell her daddy she liked girls, could she?

Licking her dry lips, Brynn looked back up at her daddy, then said, "We have a project together in school. We're sorta friends now."

"Sort of friends?" her father repeated.

"Yes, sir." Brynn shrugged. "I used to think she was mean, but she's really not."

"I'm going to ask you one question, and I want you to be completely honest with me, okay?"

"Okay."

"Are you a lesbian?"

Cassidy's sudden choked coughing broke the momentary silence following the dreaded question. Her blue eyes widened and watered, causing Brynn's mother to offer her a drink. Cassidy shook her head, mumbled that she was okay, and sank down into the couch, probably wishing it could swallow her alive.

Brynn knew her face had paled. She could feel all the life draining out of her body. That question had been coming. She knew it even before the interrogation began, and instead of sitting there wishing things could've been different for her, she immediately looked over at Laura and said, "Get out." And yet as angry as she was, her voice sounded calm, frighteningly calm.

"Laura," her mother said, "I think it would be best if you leave now."

Sorrow filled Laura's eyes, but Brynn didn't care. Even as Laura hung her head and cautiously walked out of the room, Brynn didn't care about her hurt or her pain or her sorrow. Brynn felt betrayed, and that was Laura's fault. Her former friend had crossed a line she didn't need to cross, and her mistake left Brynn and Cassidy paying the price.

"Daddy, I...."

Brynn swallowed hard as she stood from the chair. She began pacing a tight circle, like a caged animal with a need to break free. As she walked that short distance—back and forth, back and forth—she thought of an easy way to let her parents down, but there was no easy way to do it.

And when she finally resigned herself to that fact, she looked back up at her dad and said, "Yes, sir. I think I am."

If anything in the world could've crushed her, it would've been the look on her parents' faces. They looked nothing less than disappointed in her and she hated that. She'd never done anything to disappoint them—anger them, yes, but she'd never once let them down. Not until this moment.

"Get out of my house," her father said in a quiet, even voice. He didn't sound angry at all, but rather heartbroken.

Her mother didn't say a word.

"Daddy," Brynn breathed. Her legs trembled so bad she thought she might collapse right there. Tears burned beneath her eyelids, but somehow they didn't manage to break free. Her heart beat wildly inside her chest.

She looked to her mother, who only lowered her head; looked at Cassidy, who appeared just as lost as she was; then she finally turned her stare to her father, who couldn't seem to look her in the eyes.

"Daddy, please."

"I can't condone this, Brynn."

"Condone what? The way I feel?"

"The choice you made."

"I didn't make this choice, Daddy!" Brynn's voice rose to near screaming. She stabbed her finger in the air. The rims of her eyes reddened. "I can't help the way I feel. What do you want from me?"

"I want you to get out of my house."

Without a single uttered syllable, Brynn tore out of the front door and down the driveway. Cassidy called after her, chasing behind her, but Brynn didn't stop. She couldn't stop, not until she had a safe place to break down, and that place ended up being the middle of the street at the entrance to the cul-de-sac. Her knees hit the asphalt, and tears poured from her eyes.

Chapter 27

BY THE time Cassidy caught up to Brynn, her heart had shattered into a trillion pieces. She was a tough girl. There was very little that could move her, but the sight of Brynn crying helplessly in the middle of the street did it.

She eased down beside Brynn, gently rubbing a hand in small circles across her back. "Shhh. Don't cry, Brynnie. He just doesn't know how to handle it. Give him some time." A car drove by, slowing down to witness the fiasco in the middle of the usually quiet street. Cassidy shot the driver a blood-chilling glare, and the man drove off.

"Please don't cry. It'll be okay… I promise." It was a whole lot to promise, but she didn't know what else to say to calm the hysterical Brynn down. And with every loud sob that escaped Brynn, Cassidy's heart broke a little more.

For what seemed like forever, they sat there—Brynn crying her eyes out and Cassidy making every attempt to assuage her wrecked emotions. At this point, she was about ready to heft Brynn over her shoulder and carry her the short distance to her own house. At least her mother and grandmother wouldn't be half as judgmental as Brynn's parents had been. As a matter of fact, that was a pretty good idea.

Softly, she said, "Do you want to come to my house?"

"Please," Brynn somehow managed through her crying. "I don't have anywhere else to go."

"Come on, baby girl. Get up."

Cassidy helped Brynn to her feet and draped one of her slender arms around her shoulders. Acting as a support bracket, she slowly made her way around the corner to her front door. Her mother and grandmother sat outside, drinking something undoubtedly alcoholic and laughing over conversation.

"Dear gods, what happened?" Her mother rose to her feet and sprinted down the paved driveway. As usual, her grandmother followed closely behind.

"Forget what happened, come inside and get washed up," Nana said, taking Brynn's hand and leading her into the house.

Cassidy trudged up the drive, looking down at her feet the whole way and ignoring her mother's piercing stare. Once inside, Brynn disappeared into the kitchen, and Cassidy's mother walked around so Cassidy had no choice but to look at her.

"Well? What happened to Brynn? Was it that Laura girl again?" Her mother looked angry as all get-out.

"Yeah, it was. It's complicated, 'kay? Can I just go make sure Brynn's okay before I start to explain?"

"Fine, but I want answers, and so help me gods if that evil young lady did anything to hurt either of you...."

Cassidy ignored her mother's commentary and made a beeline for the kitchen, where she found Nana sitting across from Brynn, a handful of tissues in one hand and a glass of water in the other. Brynn was still crying, and for the hundredth time that evening, Cassidy didn't know what to do about it.

"What happened, child? Are you hurt?" Nana softly inquired as she pushed the glass of water toward Brynn, who just shook her head.

"It was that evil girl, Laura something," Cassidy's mom chimed in. She closed the space between the table and herself, and Cassidy followed behind.

"Did she wreck your car too?"

"No, she wrecked her life more like it," Cassidy said, standing beside Brynn's chair.

"No one has the power to wreck your life. Not in high school, anyway. Do you want to talk about it?" Nana pressed. Brynn shook her head, and Cassidy took the lead.

"She told Brynn's parents that she was a… that she's into girls."

Nana and Miranda exchanged glances, but they remained silent for a moment. Finally, they spoke at once. "Are you?" Cassidy's mom asked, while Nana simply said, "So?"

Cassidy realized neither woman made the connection that she herself was tied into the implication. To clear things up—because at this point, why shouldn't she?—she spoke up. "Yeah, she is. And so am I. I think. I mean, we think. I mean… we like each other, ya know?"

More silence. This time, the quiet dragged on for what felt like an eternity, and Brynn looked up at Cassidy, mascara-streaked eyes wide behind her pink bangs. Stares bounced around the room. No one looked directly at anyone else. It was as if no one knew exactly what to say and no one wanted to make a bad situation worse. It was the hoarse, tear-filled voice of the girl who hadn't uttered a word since her father told her to get out who finally broke the silence. The words were very simply "I love her."

Nana's wise voice gently followed that statement. "Well then, that's cause for happiness, not tears."

"Unless Cassidy doesn't feel the same way," Cassidy's mother added.

"No, I do. I totes do love her," Cassidy admitted without hesitation, and damn if it didn't feel good to finally say that out loud to the two women in her life who mattered as much as Brynn did. "But I don't know how to make this okay. Her dad kicked her out of their house."

Nana looked like someone had smacked her across the face with a religious book. To her credit, however, she simply cleared her throat and said, "That's just ignorant."

"Mom, not everyone has been in love with a woman before. Most people aren't as open-minded as I am, either," Cassidy's mom said before turning to Brynn. "You're more than welcome to stay here as long as you need to, Brynn… but I think it would be appropriate for you girls to maybe sleep on opposite ends of the bed."

Nana scoffed. "Miranda, please. Do you really think that sex is on their minds after the night they've clearly had?"

Cassidy's mother blinked and sat quietly, clearly attempting to figure out what the rules of engagement were for young lesbians. "They're teenage girls. Isn't sex always on their minds?"

Cassidy turned nine hundred shades of crimson. "Mom, we're right here, you know."

The banter bouncing back and forth was apparently the one thing Brynn needed to lighten her mood. Her lips curled, and the smile on her face pushed dimples into her rosy cheeks. It filled her eyes with the innocent sparkle Cassidy had grown to adore. It was the most beautiful, genuine smile Cassidy could've hoped for under the circumstances.

"Finally, we've got this poor girl to smile," Nana said, not a little too proudly, as if she'd accomplished the feat on her own. "Why don't you two go get washed up, and I'll call Brynn's parents to let them know she's okay."

"No!" Brynn yelled. She immediately covered her mouth and quieted her voice. "I mean, please don't. I don't think now is a good time."

"Well, they are your parents, sweetie, and you know them best. Let's leave well enough alone then and head to bed. Maybe you two can skip school tomorrow and take some time to reflect on everything that's happened," Miranda said, rising from the chair she'd taken earlier.

"Oh sure, because that's all we need is for Brynn's parents to hate us all for being liberal lesbian supporters who encourage their daughter to skip school." Nana never faltered in providing a witty comment. It helped, though. Goodness, did it help.

Cassidy kissed both her mom and grandmother goodnight and took Brynn upstairs to her bedroom. She loaned Brynn some pajamas and gave her a fresh towel, spare toothbrush, and all the hair products she could possibly need to feel at home. Twenty minutes later, they both lay freshly showered and tucked into Cassidy's bed.

"I meant what I said earlier," Brynn whispered. "About loving you and stuff."

Cassidy leaned over, pressed a tender kiss to Brynn's forehead, and said, "I know you did. So did I. Get some rest, Brynnie. Tomorrow's another day, yeah?"

"Yeah, I guess it is," Brynn said through a yawn as her eyelids fluttered closed.

Chapter 28

BRYNN woke up to the feel of a warm body at her back and arms wrapped around her. A gentle breath brushed against the nape of her neck. She almost didn't want to open her eyes, but she could feel the sunlight begging to break through her closed lids.

A lot of the night before was a blur. Emotions had raged. Things happened quickly, a little too quickly. If she'd had any rational thought at all, she might've asked her father to reconsider kicking her out. She still had months of school left, and the idea of being a homeless teen freaked her out. She didn't have a job or anything, no way to take care of herself. She'd even left her car at their house.

Thank God for Cassidy's family.

The only bright note in this whole mess was being close to Cassidy. At least with Brynn's father telling her to go, she got to spend the night in Cassidy's arms. She really did love that girl, and the more her girlfriend stepped up to help her, the more Brynn felt that love.

"You awake?" she whispered. If Cassidy hadn't woken up yet, Brynn didn't want to be the one who interrupted her sleep. After all, Cassidy had had an equally rough night as well.

"Are we still in Kansas, Toto?"

Brynn laughed hard enough to jostle her shoulders. She rolled in Cassidy's arms, and the tips of their noses brushed together. "You and your uncanny sense of humor," she said before stealing a quick kiss.

"Did Dorothy get a good night's sleep?"

"Oh my gawd, I slept like a bear in hibernation," Cassidy said on a yawn. "How about you? Did you manage to get any rest?"

"More than I've had in a while. It's weird. I think that... stuff being out in the open lifted a weight off my shoulders, and I really didn't have anything left to worry about. Well, 'cept for Daddy."

"I think you should feed your daddy to my Nana and let her handle it."

"She'll slaughter him." Brynn half laughed. "Captain Daddy and Witchy Grandma... round one."

"And our moms can exchange recipes and gardening tips in the meanwhile. How very suburban."

There was a soft tapping at the door, and Brynn eased out of Cassidy's arms, then sat up on the edge of the bed. Even though her girlfriend's mom and Nana had been completely cool last night, there was no need to push boundaries. After all, Brynn was sort of at their mercy right now, what with needing a place to crash and all.

"Come in," Cassidy called out from behind her, voice muffled by a pillow.

Nana poked her head in the door, long ringlets of salt and pepper curls falling down from the side of her smiling face. "You girls coherent yet?"

They both grumbled.

Nana laughed. "I had a thought. May I come in?"

"Sure, Nana," Cassidy said.

The sweet older lady stepped all the way into the bedroom, then closed the door behind her. She sat down on the bed next to Brynn and laid her tender, slightly wrinkled hand on Brynn's knee. "I want to take the two of you to the college today. There's a youth group there that I think will help you both out."

"Nana, I don't need help," Cassidy said with a groan.

"Well, maybe Brynn would like to talk to people who have been in her same situation. Don't you want to go with her, be supportive of her?" Nana gave Brynn a wink.

"Well, when you put it that way…."

"I think that would be nice," Brynn said.

Nana gently patted Brynn's knee before standing from the bed. "Well, you two get ready, and we'll head on out. Lunch is on me."

"Thanks, Nana," both girls said in unison.

The door closed, and Brynn looked back at Cassidy. She had already burrowed back down under the covers, head hidden by a pillow. Brynn stood up and as per her normal routine, started for the bathroom, but a thought stopped her. She turned back toward the bed. "Um, I don't have a change of clothes…."

Cassidy peeked over the blanket, blue eyes shining in the sunlight streaming into the room. "No worries. You can just borrow something of mine. Rummage through my closet and see what you might wanna wear."

"You sure?"

"Mhm," Cassidy mumbled.

Brynn went over to Cassidy's closet and stepped inside what could've easily been a small bedroom. She looked over the rainbow of colors Cassidy had hanging in the row of shirts and blouses. She immediately went to the darker colors, not that Cassidy had much to choose from in the way of emo trends. What she ended up choosing was so outside the spectrum of her norm, she couldn't believe she'd chosen it for herself.

The shirt was a pale green, almost seafoam, and went well with her cotton-candy-pink hair. She grabbed a pair of faded jeans. "Cassidy, tell me if this is okay," she called from the closet.

Cassidy finally stumbled out of bed, blonde hair a beautiful disaster around her angelic face. She padded to the closet, where a half smile pinched her cheeks. "I like that color on you. And you chose it all on your own without even looking at the black stuff!"

"Wait, there's black stuff?" Brynn said teasingly as she turned back toward the rows and rows of name-brand clothes. Cassidy grabbed her arm, and when Brynn spun around to face her girlfriend again, Cassidy had the most gorgeous smile on her face.

In an airy rush, Brynn said, "I was only kidding."

"So was I. There really isn't any black stuff." Cassidy laughed, pulling Brynn closer into her personal space.

Biting her bottom lip, Brynn looked down, instantly noticing the hint of cleavage just barely peeking up from Cassidy's pink cami. With each breath Cassidy took, her breasts rose, then slowly lowered. It was like being hypnotized by one of those swinging-watch things. Brynn couldn't look away.

"I... I...," she stammered, all rational thought vanished.

Cassidy's soft voice filled the quiet space of the closet as she teased. "You're always looking at my boobs. I think it's time you got a little more than just a view through a pajama shirt."

Before Brynn could react, Cassidy stripped away the cami and stood unabashed before her, perky breasts exposed for Brynn's eyes. She took a few steps closer, enticing Brynn even further.

Brynn was completely speechless, and her eyes were as wide as saucers. She wanted to touch Cassidy, wanted to know what that radiant, tanned flesh felt like against her palm, but God help her, she was terrified. She kept worrying her bottom lip as Cassidy stood there staring. Her heart fluttered, and her pulse started to race. Her hands were probably trembling, but she couldn't really think about shaking fingers with the half-naked girl right in front of her.

"Cassidy, I—"

Her voice was instantly silenced the moment she felt Cassidy's hands over hers, lifting her arms until her fingers found the soft, supple curves of Cassidy's breasts. Brynn looked down at her cupped hands, then up at Cassidy's serene, smiling face, then back down at her hands. She couldn't believe this was happening, and someone kill her now if she ended up panicking over this.

"Don't freak out, Brynnie. It's natural. They're just boobs." Cassidy Rivers, ever the casual one. Brynn's heart was in her throat, beating through her ears, and Cassidy was the textbook definition of calm, cool, and collected. "Let your body guide you. Touch 'em. Squish 'em. Kiss 'em. Do whatever you want to do."

"I don't know what to do," Brynn said. "I… I…."

Don't panic. Don't panic.

"They're pretty," she nervously offered.

"So explore them. Explore me," Cassidy said, still as calm as the moment she'd woken up. Her own hands cupped Brynn's, fingers gently pushing her palms against Cassidy's tender flesh.

Cassidy leaned in enough for their lips to touch, a teasing touch, nothing more than a gentle brush. Brynn closed her eyes and opened her mouth wider. She wanted a real kiss, a kiss like the boys and girls at school shared when no one was looking. And the moment she thought about Cassidy's lips embracing hers, her girlfriend took over, and Brynn's mouth belonged to her.

She was so lost in that deep, amazing kiss, she missed the moment Cassidy released her hands. She was oblivious to the fact her fingers were tenderly waving over the mounds of pliable flesh Brynn had always seen covered by frilly lace or soft fabric. In fact, she wasn't aware of Cassidy's hands until the moment she felt that warmth sliding up the back of her shirt.

The air from the vent above them brushed over Brynn's exposed back. She broke the kiss to the sound of Cassidy whimpering. "Maybe we should get dressed before we get caught," Brynn suggested, voice hoarse.

"Hmmm?" Cassidy's eyes fluttered open as she withdrew her hands from Brynn's body. "Oh yeah. Dressed. Caught. Right," she breathed, much to Brynn's amusement. It appeared that somewhere along the line, Miss Calm Cool and Collected had lost her bearings as well.

"Okay… so, uh, that outfit looks perfect. Erm, you need a bra, though," Cassidy pointed out, gaze locked on Brynn's chest for a moment before she blinked hard and spun around, disappearing from the closet. When she reemerged, there were two delicate, very expensive-looking bras in her hands. "I dunno what you prefer, so I brought you one of each. Padded or just underwire."

"My boobs aren't as big as yours, I promise. Maybe the padded one?"

A nod later, Cassidy handed over the pale pink, padded bra in her left hand. She stood there for a moment, a silent question filling her azure gaze before she asked, "You want me to turn around again or…?"

"Stay."

"Pinky, I wasn't planning on leaving. Just turning around in case you were still shy."

"I just had my hands on your boobs. I think we're past shy now…."

"Yeah, but those were *my* boobs."

"Then how's this?"

Oh God, what am I doing? Brynn thought as she slowly lifted her shirt over her head and let it drop to the floor. She didn't have a body as utterly perfect as Cassidy's. She didn't have Cassidy's charisma or confidence, and there she was pretending to be something she couldn't pull off. She just couldn't do sexy. It didn't work for her.

This time around, it was Cassidy's eyes that widened. Her girlfriend looked starstruck, as if she'd seen her favorite celebrity standing inside her closet. Her heart-shaped lips parted to reveal a pink tongue swiping across her lower lip. Just as her hands raised and she took a step forward, Nana's voice stopped her.

"Are you two ready to go yet?" Cassidy's grandmother called from just outside the bedroom door.

Cassidy rolled her eyes and huffed, undoubtedly in frustration. "Of *course* she interrupts when it's my turn," she grumbled.

Chapter 29

A MALE couple ambled past Cassidy, entering the classroom Nana had directed them to. Once she stepped inside, she looked around while Brynn reached out and held her hand. The room wasn't anything like she'd been expecting. There were bright paintings on the walls and ceramic sculptures set up on shelves. Easels stood to one side, with a row of cans holding paintbrushes beside them. There were a few other same-sex couples—or what she guessed were couples—sitting across the space, a few per table.

Admittedly, this kind of thing made Cassidy nervous. Not because she felt uncomfortable with who she was, but she didn't need the world staring at her as if she had some dirty little secret that was only to be revealed in the small confines of like-minded groups. Maybe that was Nana's genes more than anything.

Nana led them to a rectangular table, empty save for three plastic, dark blue chairs. Brynn immediately sat down in the middle seat, leaving Cassidy and Nana to take up either side. A few other people came walking in, and with every person who sat down and looked over at her, Cassidy felt her unease grow a little more. She wanted to stand up and tell them there wasn't anything wrong with them. She felt like she should explain that the world was cruel to everyone, not just same-sex couples. Then she realized she was eighteen years old and most of the people there were a bit older than her, so maybe she didn't really have it all figured out just yet.

Some lady dressed in a plain black T-shirt and black skinny jeans stood at the front of the classroom, where she introduced herself as Michelle Swanson, head of the art department at the university and program director for the LGBT group. She had a warm smile and a soft voice, and Cassidy immediately liked her demeanor.

Until she asked if any new people wanted to introduce themselves.

Nuh-uh. Cassidy was so not gonna stand up in a room full of people and be all *"Hi, I'm Cassidy Rivers and I'm a lesbian."* Nope. It wasn't gonna happen. That kind of stuff was for people in rehab groups or those who needed a psychologist to sit around in a circle with them and share feelings. For what might have been the first time in her life, Cassidy sank down into the chair and wished she could disappear.

Brynn, on the other hand, must have channeled all of Cassidy's bravado. Pinky stood up, albeit reluctantly, and introduced herself. "Hi, I, um… I'm Brynn Michaels." She paused, and Cassidy watched in amazement as that lovely shade of rosy red filled Brynn's cheeks. "I'm seventeen and I, um… well, I guess I'm a lesbian."

Everyone in the room let out a startling "Hi, Brynn."

Brynn glanced down at Cassidy, who cleared her throat, then gently shook her head. She might have sunk a bit lower into the chair too. Brynn ignored her and gave her wrist a little tug.

Lovely. Pinky had found her voice. Well, at least she was proud of her for doing what Cassidy'd sworn not to do. Since Brynn had the lead, Cassidy might as well follow. She rose from her seat, smiled shyly, and said, "I'm Cassidy Rivers. Eighteen, totally a lesbian, and Brynn's girlfriend."

There. That wasn't so bad, right?

Right.

The people in the room once again sounded out in a welcoming "Hi, Cassidy," and before she knew it, Brynn took her seat again, with Cassidy planting her butt back down. Nana leaned over and whispered that she was going to go outside and make a few phone calls, then exited the room. Probably to give them some space and a little more room to be themselves.

Cassidy looked over at Brynn, still at a loss over what to do at this type of thing.

THE woman in black—the head of whatever, Brynn couldn't remember at the moment—started talking about everything the school had going on in terms of LGBT student affairs. None of that had anything to do with Brynn, and she was still so unsettled and nervous about even being there, she couldn't really concentrate on what the woman was saying.

The lady then went on talking about community events. Some of them got Brynn's attention. They sounded fun for the most part, but then she offered the floor to the people who'd come out, said they could discuss whatever they wanted to, and if anyone wanted private counseling, mentors were available.

Brynn started to wonder why Nana had brought them out to this thing. She was too scared to raise her hand and ask questions, even though she had a million and twelve of them. The idea had kind of been for her and Cassidy to travel this road together, to learn and grow from each other. Not a bunch of strangers. But there they sat, staring straight ahead, but clinging to each other's hands.

"Hi," a soft, petite but somehow masculine voice said from beside them. Cassidy and Brynn both turned their heads and found a tall, skinny—too skinny—guy sitting down beside them. "I'm John," he said, offering his hand. Cassidy was the one brave enough to sit up and give it a shake. "I'm a mentor, so I'm here to listen if you need to talk."

"Cool," Cassidy said. "Can you answer questions too? 'Cause I think we might have a couple… or twenty."

"I can," John said with a smile as he sat back in his chair. He crossed his legs and folded his hands in his lap. "Anything you want to talk about."

"Are you out?" Brynn blurted, making air quotes when she said the word "out." Cassidy looked over like Brynn had lost her freaking mind.

"Yes, I am." John laughed lightly. "I came out to my parents when I was fifteen."

That must've had Cassidy curious, because she piped up and asked, "How did it go? If you don't mind me asking."

"I don't. And it went better than I thought it would. My mom hugged me and said she loved me. My dad didn't take it as well, but he didn't freak out completely. He just needed some time to warm up to the idea of his only son being gay, I think."

"What did he do?" Brynn asked.

"He didn't say anything. In fact, he didn't speak to me for a few days. He made himself pretty scarce to everyone in the house. Then one day, I was sitting at the kitchen table doing my homework, and he sat down across from me. I was terrified. I thought he was going to yell and scream and tell me to get the hell out of his house."

Brynn's throat tightened. Just hearing John repeat what had happened to her took her back to last night. She could still see the disappointment in her father's eyes, and she could hear the disgust in his voice. It sent a chill down her spine, a chill so cold it made her shiver.

"What did he do?" Cassidy asked, tightening her fingers around Brynn's hand.

"He told me he loved me. Said he may not agree with my lifestyle, but I was his blood, and he loved me no matter what. I can't begin to tell you how relieved I was."

If only Brynn's father could've reacted the same way.

She lowered her head the second she felt the sting in her eyes. The idea of those people, those strangers, seeing her cry hurt almost as badly as reliving that horrible, hateful moment with her father. The more she thought about what happened between them, and the more she wished she'd had it as easy as Cassidy, or even John for that matter, the harder it became to fight the tears.

Cassidy sat up and said, "Brynn's dad kicked her out last night when he found out."

Brynn would have freaking killed her for saying that out loud, but she couldn't really be mad at Cassidy for trying to help. Even less so when her girlfriend leaned over and pressed a chaste kiss to Brynn's cheek and whispered, "We're here for you to try and get solutions. Don't be afraid, 'kay?"

Brynn nodded and kept trying to hold back the now slow stream of tears that burned her cheeks.

John released a soft sigh and shook his head. He unlaced his fingers and placed a hand over Brynn's, patting it consolingly. "I'm sorry to hear that. Truly. If that happened just last night, give him some time to warm up to the idea. All parents handle it differently. Some are accepting, others, not so much. Do you have somewhere to stay in the meanwhile?"

"She's staying at my house. My mom's okay with my sexual preference." Lucky Cassidy. If Brynn's mother could at least accept it, maybe it wouldn't be so heart-wrenching. But her mom hadn't. She'd just sat there, looking as disappointed as her daddy had.

"Thankfully there's that." John reached into his back pocket and pulled out a stainless steel card holder, from where he retrieved a business card and leaned over to hand it to Cassidy. "My phone numbers and e-mail address are there. Brynn, if at any time you think you might benefit from having me speak to your parents, please don't hesitate to call me. Also, if either of you have questions, I'm always available."

"Thank you," Brynn said, trying to control the tremble in her voice. "I, um… I think I want to go now."

Clearly Cassidy didn't have to be told twice. She sprang from her seat as if someone had sparked a rocket under her butt. "Okay, we can go now. John, thank you for your help and for talking to us," she said as she offered an extended arm to the mentor.

"It's no problem at all," John said as he shook her hand. "That's what we're here for."

He gave Brynn a sorrowful smile, and that's all Brynn could stand. She lowered her head and walked away from them both, not slowing down for Cassidy to catch up. She just needed to get out of there… now!

Chapter 30

By THE time they made it to the car, Brynn had somewhat managed to stifle her tears. Maybe for Nana's sake more than anything. Whatever the case, Cassidy's grandmother hadn't asked any questions when she'd seen Brynn's puffy red eyes. Another point for Nana's timing.

In the car, Cassidy worried about Brynn. Normally she'd tell her to chillax and remind her that everything would be okay. She could hold her hand or kiss her tears away, but it didn't seem like that was what Brynn needed. Frankly, Cassidy didn't think what Brynn needed had much to do with her at all, and so it left her rather quiet for the ride home. She did, however, still hold Brynn's hand and sit super extra close to her, just so Pinky could feel the warmth of her presence at her side.

The ride back home seemed to take a whole lot longer than the ride to the college had taken. On their way there, they'd stopped for lunch at a small, outdoor cafe. They'd laughed the entire time. They'd smiled over silly things, and everything had been so freaking fine. If Cassidy could take that same mentality and channel it into Brynn, she would, because her girlfriend was totally not fine at the moment. Actually, she was everything *but* fine, and the long car ride didn't help to ease the discomfort Brynn obviously still felt.

Cassidy resorted to counting the miles left to go on the car's GPS. The digital odometer ticked by, moving at a snail's pace. *Five miles....*

Brynn's sniffling made her jump. She reached into her Fendi purse and fished around for a tissue before handing it to her.

"Thank you" was all Brynn managed.

"You're welcome" was all Cassidy could reply with.

The tension inside the car was almost unbearable, but she still refrained from saying anything just to fill the silence. Sometimes less was more, even though she rarely adopted that mentality.

Four miles....

"So, Brynn. If you're going to be staying over again tonight, what would you like to eat? I can make anything you like." Nana to the rescue. Thank freaking gawd.

Cassidy turned her attention to Brynn, who locked their gazes for a fleeting moment. Even with her eyes all red and puffy, even with her nose all swollen and her cheeks all blotchy from crying, she was still the prettiest girl Cassidy had ever seen, and it broke her heart that not only was Brynn hurting, but she couldn't do squat about it either.

"Anything is fine with me, thank you," Brynn said. Her voice wavered, splitting toward the end of her statement on a soft sob.

Crack. Shatter. Break. Break. Ugh. Cassidy could almost hear the breaking of Pinky's heart. It was horrible.

Three miles....

"Well, what's your favorite dish? Better yet, do you like macaroni and cheese? I make a mean macaroni and cheese. It's got four different types of cheese in it... and bacon too, if you're okay with that," Nana said, as she turned the volume down a few notches on the radio.

Once more, Brynn simply said, "That's fine. Thank you," and Cassidy figured she could either take the reins of this conversation or they'd be stuck listening to a very long list of Nana's best dishes.

"Nana, that sounds perfect. Maybe you can make some biscuits too, and some lemonade if you have the time. Tell me how you make the lemonade again. I always forget."

Brynn couldn't say Cassidy didn't do anything for her, because she'd just taken one major hit for team Pinky. She knew how to make her grandmother's lemonade. She'd been in the kitchen with her, watching her make it for as long as she could remember. Luckily, Nana began to rattle off the process anyway.

"Oh, that's simple and so refreshing, isn't it? It's four cups of cold water—the water *has* to be cold—followed by the juice of six lemons. Now, the trick is to hand squeeze them. You can't use one of those fancy juicers or the bits of seed will end up in there and change the taste. You'll also need a simple syrup, which consists of one cup of granulated sugar, boiled down into one cup of water. You have to let that cool down first, before adding it to the lemonade."

Two miles....

Nana continued. "Finally, you mix it all together with a wooden spoon. No whisks! Whisks will make it frothy, and no one likes frothy lemonade. Add some ice cubes at the end and a few slices of lemon, and you've got yourself a great glass of lemonade."

"Oh right. The whisk. I always forget about the whisk," Cassidy replied mindlessly as she stared out of the window. Brynn gave her hand a little squeeze and she took that as a thank you from Pinky.

"No whisks! They're horrible for stirring lemonade. The pulp becomes mush, and the sugar gets... well, I already said it gets frothy."

"Eww, frothy lemonade. The horror."

Nana looked into the rearview mirror at the same time Cassidy's gaze rose to meet hers. The no-nonsense glare her grandmother was shooting back at her silently warned her of the horrors that frothy lemonade did indeed hold. Then, probably as torture for mocking her adamant dislike of lemonade froth, Nana turned up Tom Jones.

One mile....

For that last mile, Cassidy's thoughts turned back to Brynn, sitting in absolute silence at her side. She leaned over and again pressed a kiss to her girlfriend's cheek. She whispered that she loved her, which finally made the edges of Brynn's mouth turn upward in the slightest of smiles, and Cassidy took that as a small victory. She was further rewarded when Brynn whispered back, "I love you too." It was barely audible, but it was enough to make Cassidy smile.

That content smile lasted all of five seconds, derailed by Nana asking, "Whose car could that be?"

Cassidy looked up, having been too wrapped up in trying to make Brynn happy to realize they'd made it into Majestic Hills, around the cul-de-sac, and were now slowing down as they neared Cassidy's house. When she saw what Nana was talking about, she recognized the minivan from the driveway at Brynn's house just as Brynn gasped and said, "Oh no."

And those darn zombies began to munch away at her insides again.

Nana glanced back after pulling her car in beside the minivan. Her stare questioned them both, but she said nothing. Finally, Brynn said, "That's my mom's car," as she unbuckled her seat belt with shaky hands.

"Oh, wonderful. I have a few things I'd like to talk to her about," Nana said before bolting out of the car as fast as a woman in her mid-sixties could.

She started toward the house, walking with a determined gait. Cassidy recognized the impending horrors that would soon befall whatever member of the Michaels household might be sitting inside her house, so she darted out of the car and started after Nana.

"Nana!" she hissed. "They're, like, super religious and super strict! Don't go in there guns blazing in defense of lesbian rights, 'kay?" Her grandmother merely cocked a shaped brow. "Please?" Cassidy added.

The please must have done it because Nana sighed and nodded stubbornly. "Fine, but only for Brynn's sake. Between you and me—" Her wise, steel-blue gaze shot up, probably making sure Brynn wasn't within earshot. "—any parent who kicks their kid out of their home just for being gay makes them butt monkeys in my book."

"Butt monkeys. Duly noted, Nana. Now can we please just go see what they want?"

Brynn finally made it over to stand at Cassidy's side just as her grandmother nodded again and opened the front door.

With the nonchalance only Nana could pull off, she stepped into the foyer, and in a tone dripping with sweet charm, she said, "Miranda, the girls and I are home. We had a *lovely* time today. Oh, you should have seen how they were laughing and smiling together."

Cassidy swore Nana was a Spartan in her past life, because there was no other person more ready to wage war than she was. All in a diplomatic, sort of in-your-face way. Thank gawd her grandmother was in town. She didn't think she could survive this fiasco without Nana's sage wisdom and easy-going attitude toward her newfound sexuality.

She even thought she heard a quiet giggle coming from Brynn, but that could have just been her imagination, because when she looked over at her girlfriend, her eyes were wide, and her already light complexion seemed a whiter shade of pale. Cassidy immediately clasped her hand around Brynn's. She laced their fingers together and gave a small squeeze, attempting to channel some confidence into her.

The tone of her mother's voice told Cassidy that things might not be as bad as she originally thought. She knew a lot of things, but most of all, she knew the different pitches of her mom's voice. If Brynn's parents were in there having a heart attack, then there would've been a slight edge to her mother's speech. Nope, this tone was… calm.

"That's great, Mom. I'm in the living room with Brynn's mother. Come say hello."

Nana, Brynn, and Cassidy all exchanged looks. Brynn took a visible deep breath, her chest rising and falling. Cassidy kept her viselike grip on Brynn's hand, and Nana offered her a gentle pat on the shoulder before whispering, "Don't worry, kiddo. We're here for you," and taking Brynn's other hand in hers. Together, they walked toward the sunny living room.

For Cassidy, it felt like walking *The Green Mile*, so she couldn't fathom what Brynn must be going through at the moment. She expected Brynn to release her hand the minute she saw her mother, but Pinky did anything but. She actually held on a little tighter, white-knuckling Cassidy's fingers until she felt the tips start to tingle.

Point one for team Pinky.

Cassidy walked into the living room with her head held high and her dainty shoulders squared. While Brynn might be intimidated by her family, Cassidy was proud of who she was, and there wasn't a close-minded woman in the world who would change that. She locked gazes with Mrs. Michaels, who sat on the large loveseat opposite from the couch. A glass of ice water accompanied a napkin in her left hand. She looked like she'd been crying.

It was the same worn-down expression Cassidy's mother donned when her father up and left them, taking his Bose sound system in one arm and a suitcase full of designer clothes in the other. The same sorrow-filled look to her eyes. The same questions probably clouding her thoughts. Why had this happened to her? What had she done? How could she fix it? The situations were on opposite ends of the spectrum, but the results were the same.

Cassidy opened her mouth to speak but was promptly interrupted by Nana, who broke their little circle of strength and walked over to offer Mrs. Michaels a hand.

"I'm Sylvia Donovan, Miranda's mother and Cassidy's grandmother. Your daughter is a beautiful young lady, Mrs. Michaels. Both inside and out."

Brynn's mom smiled politely, gave a small flick of her wrist, and said, "Thank you. That's what I'm here about," before turning her gaze to Brynn. "Do you two mind having a seat? There are some things that I need to speak to Brynn about, and I was hoping you would sit in as well, Cassidy."

Brynn nervously looked at Cassidy. Cassidy gave a small shrug and nodded. She led Brynn to the couch, where they sat down beside one another. Neither one released the other's hand, and neither one spoke.

Cassidy's mother sat on the opposite end of the couch from them, smiling and picking at a fingernail. Brynn's mother shifted and Nana… well, Nana cleared her throat, sat back in the lounge chair she'd taken up residence in, and said, "Well, this isn't *The View*, so let's get on with it, shall we? These girls have had a long day."

Chapter 31

"I BROUGHT your laptop, phone, and some clothes to you. Your favorite hoodie is in your backpack," Brynn's mom said. Her voice had a nervous waver to it. "Your school books are all—"

"Wait," Brynn interrupted, bolting up from her spot on the couch beside Cassidy. "Are you trying to tell me I can't come home?"

"Brynn...." Her mother lowered her head. She sniffled once, wrung her hands, and then looked up at Brynn again. There was so much sadness in her eyes Brynn almost didn't want to be mad at her... almost. "Your father doesn't agree with what you've chosen."

"Chosen? Chosen!" Brynn tightened her jaw and crossed her arms over her chest. "You think I chose this? Do you honestly think I would willingly choose something so freaking hard? So scary? I can't help that every time I look at Cassidy I want to kiss her. I can't help wanting to be around her. I've never felt that way about a boy."

"Maybe you just haven't met the right boy yet," her mom quietly offered, as if she wasn't really sure she should be saying what she did.

At that point, Brynn saw Cassidy jump up from the couch, but Nana must've reached over and pulled her back down because she didn't stay on her feet long. Brynn felt something prickle on her neck, making the fine hairs at her nape stand on end. She glanced over her shoulder, back to her girlfriend, and saw Cassidy staring daggers at her mother. The fizzle of energy grew stronger the longer Brynn stood there without taking up for herself, as if Cassidy's powers were totally ready to take over.

Brynn looked back at her mom and said, "There won't be a right boy. Ever. I love Cassidy."

"Brynn, you're seventeen years old. You don't know what love is yet."

"Obviously, I know better than you and Daddy."

"Brynn Michaels!"

"Okay. All right." Nana stood, pressing her palms to the air to back everyone down. Brynn didn't know if Nana was taking charge for her sake or Cassidy's, because the more Brynn's mom spoke, the more Brynn became aware of her very witchy girlfriend. "How about we take a step back and look at this a little more rationally?"

Nana shot a glance at Brynn. Brynn lowered her head. Then she turned that same commanding stare on Cassidy, and the fizzle of energy filling the room immediately retreated. Nana looked to Cassidy's mom, who gave her a curt nod, as if giving her the go-ahead to keep heading down the path she'd started on.

"Mrs. Michaels," Nana said. "I think you might need a little guidance on this. Now, don't take this as an insult or anything, but it's sorta hard to know what's going on in a homosexual child's head when they first realize how they feel. I would suggest talking to parents who have been through this with their kids before you try to have a talk with Brynn about it. Because frankly, you're coming off a bit judgmental and ignorant."

"Mom!" Cassidy's mother gasped.

Cassidy smirked.

Brynn sunk down in the couch. Unfortunately, she didn't have her faithful hoodie to hide behind this time.

"I don't think name-calling is conducive to this situation," Brynn's mother stoically offered.

"Oh, I'm not calling names," Nana said. "If I was calling names, I would've said—"

"Mother!" Cassidy's mom popped up from her seat. "Mrs. Michaels, forgive my mother. We think she's going senile."

"I'm not senile," Nana declared. "I just think the woman could be better informed. Don't you, Miranda?"

"Okay. Fine," Brynn's mother said as she stood from her seat. "Help me be better informed. Contrary to what you might think, I only want what's best for my daughter."

"That's a great answer," Nana said with a smile. "Tell you what. The place where I took Brynn and Cassidy today also hosts a local PFLAG chapter—"

"PFLAG?" Brynn's mother frowned.

"Parents, friends, and family of lesbians and gays." She paused, apparently waiting for some response from Brynn's mother. Besides a silent "Oh," Brynn's mother didn't say a word. "The people in that group are good people. Some I've known half my life. They've all been through, or their parents went through, the same thing you are. Maybe they can offer you a little insight, help you make rational decisions? Your husband is welcome to go too."

"Right now, I don't think he's interested," Brynn's mother confessed.

The words ripped Brynn's heart right out of her chest. Save for the thumping of her pulse in her temples, Brynn didn't hear another sound after that. Was her father so close-minded he didn't want to understand how she felt? Had she really disappointed him so badly he didn't want to ever see her again?

Was being a lesbian really that bad?

Brynn lowered her head and began fidgeting with her shirt. If she counted the stitches at the hem, maybe she would forget how badly this whole situation hurt; maybe she wouldn't cry again. She thought if she could just keep her mind busy, the pain of letting her parents down wouldn't be so hard to bear.

"I would like to go to this meeting," Brynn's mother said, and Brynn's head darted straight up.

That Witch!

"Really?" Brynn breathlessly asked.

"Yes, really. Brynn, I *do* want to understand. Even if I don't like it, I want to understand how you feel, and I don't want to alienate you. You're my firstborn, sweetie. I love you."

"I love you too, Mom."

"That's great," Nana said with a glowing smile. "They meet on Thursday nights. Would you like me to go with you so you won't be alone?"

"We'll both go," Cassidy's mom offered.

"Thank you," Brynn's mother replied.

So maybe this whole being out thing could turn around. Maybe her parents would come to understand. That wasn't too much to hope for, was it?

Brynn felt Cassidy's hand on hers again. She found Cassidy giving her the softest, calmest smile. There was a new feeling of hope and light, not the tense, angry fizzle she'd felt from Cassidy before. She genuinely had the support system she'd so desperately wanted, and that seemed to make dealing with everything a lot easier.

"Why don't we give Brynn and her mother a moment alone?" Cassidy's mom suggested.

No. She really, *really* needed to keep holding Cassidy's hand. She needed it so bad her fingers instinctively tightened around her girlfriend's. *Please don't go. Please don't go.*

"Everything will be fine," Cassidy whispered. "I'll be right upstairs waiting for you."

Cassidy leaned over and kissed Brynn on the cheek. The feel of her soft, strawberry-scented lips against Brynn's warm skin made Brynn close her eyes. Reluctantly, she let go of Cassidy's hand, and only then did she realize her palm was sweating.

She watched as the three women she now considered her family left her alone with her mother. At first, Brynn couldn't make herself look up at the woman who'd given her life. She feared seeing the hurt

173

and sorrow in her mother's eyes. She feared the disappointment. But she didn't have to look up. The cushion beside her dipped down, and she felt her mother's arms around her, then she was being pulled into a hug.

"Sweetie," her mother said, "we'll get through this. Don't you worry, okay? Miranda says you can stay here as long as you need to, and I'm working on your father. He's just... scared, okay?"

"And I'm not?" Brynn blurted, raising her head to meet her mother's stare again. "You have no idea how scary this is for me. It feels right to be with Cassidy, to see her the way I do. And yet, I can't help feeling like I'm doing wrong because of everything I was taught. Mom, I can't help how I feel about her. I really can't."

Her mother didn't say a word, and maybe that was strictly for the sake of not arguing.

The hug loosened, and Brynn sat back on the couch. Things felt... awkward, to say the least. She didn't know what to say to her mom and how to act. She wanted everything to be normal again, but it appeared "normal" wouldn't happen anytime soon. Well, at least her mother had taken the first step, and that alone was better than anything Brynn expected to happen. That alone showed potential.

"I'm going to head back home," her mother said before kissing Brynn's forehead. "Get some rest, and I'll see you Thursday night." Brynn nodded. "I love you, honey."

"I love you too, Mom."

Brynn watched as her mother left the room. She hugged herself tightly. Even though she knew better, it felt like her mother was walking away from her for good. It made that tiny flutter of pain in her chest grow stronger. What she wouldn't give to be going back to her own home. Not that she didn't love spending time with Cassidy and her family. It just wasn't the same.

At the foot of the couch, on the floor, sat her backpack and another bag probably packed with clothes. Seeing them there hurt, but Brynn tried to make herself not read into it too much. Things *would* go back to normal. Eventually, she would be welcomed into her home again. As long as she kept telling herself that, she didn't feel so lost and hopeless.

She grabbed the bags from the floor, then headed into the kitchen. She found Cassidy and her matriarchs sitting around the table with a single blue candle lit in the center. She smelled some sort of incense, though she couldn't put a name to the scent.

"What are you guys doing?" she asked.

"The blue candle is for healing," Cassidy's mom said.

"And the eucalyptus is as well," Nana added.

"I don't normally do this crap, but they thought it would be a good idea...," Cassidy said with a shrug.

"Thank you—" Brynn smiled. "—for everything."

Chapter 32

WAKING up with Pinky was something Cassidy could get used to. It wasn't even so much the feeling of waking up with her girlfriend or her mom being so cool about it all, but it was like having her best friend living with her. What girl wouldn't totally love that? Plus, she was elated to have her car back. The rental was okay, but she loved her car. She loved being able to drive Brynn to school even more.

"Green light," Brynn said from the passenger seat, stirring Cassidy from her reverie. She smiled over at her and punched the gas pedal.

"What's got you smiling like that?" Brynn asked.

"Just thinking of how awesome it is to have you at my house. I mean, it sucks about your dad and everything, but it could be worse, ya know?" *Ugh. Another red light.* It was a conspiracy to keep her from zooming into her usual parking spot at school and showing off her shiny car to that cow, Laura, sans her hideous artwork.

"It's pretty bad, right? What could *possibly* be worse?"

Cassidy frowned slightly. "Um, well it could be a whole lot worse. My mom could've freaked and kicked us both out. Nana could not be in town to help guide your mom. Your mom could totally not have even bothered to try and understand. Don't you think all that's worse?"

"Yeah. You're right. I wasn't thinking about all that."

"You gotta look at the cup half full, my little emo queen," Cassidy said with another playful grin.

Finally, a steady stream of green lights had her zipping through town on a direct path to the school. By the time she cleared the gates of the Majestic Hills High parking lot, she was practically bouncing in her seat.

She cut the engine, reached back for her large Burberry handbag and folder, and sprang the seatbelt free. "School time!" she declared happily, eliciting a curious quirked brow from Brynn.

Pinky didn't say anything, just leaned back, grabbed her own backpack, and slowly exited the car. Her pink head bobbed up just as Cassidy looked over to see her friend Tara's Escalade pulling up beside them. She thought about going over to say hi, and that's when she realized the extent of her weird joy.

Cassidy didn't ever approach anyone just to say hi. Matter of fact, Cassidy never approached anyone, period. People were always coming up to her with greetings and salutations, presents and gossip. Somewhere along the line, something changed. And while it momentarily confused her, she decided some changes simply needed to be made.

She walked around the back of her car, smiling at Brynn, who stood at the passenger side, between both vehicles. Tara stood with the hatch of her SUV open, digging through books and piles of clothes.

"Hi, Tara," Cassidy said, coming to stand beside the brunette.

Tara's hazel eyes widened slightly, sculpted brows shooting up for just a second before she must have realized she looked like a deer in headlights and wiped the expression clean, replacing it with a smile.

"Hi, Cassidy. Are you okay? You were absent yesterday."

"Oh yeah, I was fine. Just had some family stuff to deal with."

"Oh, okay. Um, glad you're okay," Tara said, glancing over at Brynn before looking back at Cassidy. "Have... have you heard the, uh...." Those doe eyes looked down at the Mary Jane shoes adorning her feet, and Tara sighed. "Do you know what's being said about you?"

Cassidy almost snorted. She'd been waiting for Laura to start rumors, knew it would happen eventually. While she was prepared for ways to handle Laura, she wasn't so sure Brynn had it in her to deal with even more disappointment and embarrassment.

Cassidy looked at Brynn. She stood there, white-knuckling the straps of her backpack and intently peering back at her through the ever-present part in her pink bangs. Obviously, she was listening to the conversation, so Cassidy decided to approach it in the most aloof manner she knew how.

"Don't tell me. Let me guess...." She looked up at the blue sky, pretending to be lost in thought for a moment, tapping the tip of her slender finger at her chin. "I'm a lesbian."

It wasn't a question.

Tara nodded shyly, glancing away for a moment before turning back to Cassidy with a small smile. "It's cool with me if you are, you know? I mean, it's none of my business... or anyone's really, but if you are, it doesn't mean anything."

While Cassidy wasn't really looking for approval, she quickly realized she much preferred Tara's reaction over some judgmental sneer or a sideways, disapproving stare. Hell, she was even smiling—genuinely, at that—back at Tara.

"Thanks, Tara. That's really cool of you."

"You're welcome," she promptly replied, perking up a bit. "The whole cheer squad is cool with it too, so don't worry, 'kay? I hafta get to class, but I'll see you at practice later."

Whoa. The whole cheer squad knows?

Wednesday had just proven to be a little more challenging than Cassidy originally prepared for. Tara was cool, but were the other cheerleaders *really* all okay with changing in a locker room with a lesbian?

Probably not.

"Um, okay. Thanks again, Tara. See you later."

"You bet," Tara said. She closed the hatch and turned to walk away but stopped for a moment in between cars and smiled at Pinky. "Hi, Brynn. I didn't see you there. Love your outfit."

Would wonders never cease?

If Tara were dressed in a Klingon costume and had just spoken in some far-out language, Brynn couldn't have looked more surprised. "I… uh… hi, Tara… and thanks…."

"Sure thing. See you guys around."

Tara bounced off toward the school building, leaving Cassidy and Brynn standing there, exchanging *WTF* faces. Brynn closed the gap between them, stalking over to the rear end of Tara's massive SUV.

Thumbing over her shoulder in the general direction Tara had just bounced off to, Brynn asked, "Okay, seriously, did that just happen?"

"Erm, yeah, it did. Did you hear what she said about the cheer squad being okay with it? I dunno. I find that hard to believe," Cassidy said as she took Tara's lead and turned around to head toward school, all prior thoughts of rubbing her car in Laura's face temporarily forgotten.

"Cassidy," Brynn huffed. "You're missing the point. What if the whole school knows?"

"What if they do? Is it really all that bad, Brynn?"

She understood why Brynn wanted to keep it a secret. She knew her girlfriend wasn't comfortable with attention, that she preferred to just blend in the crowd or disappear right into it. But on the other hand, this was all new to her, too, and she didn't think hiding it was the best way to approach their new relationship. Especially since their parents already knew.

"I don't care if anyone knows anymore," Cassidy admitted. "According to you, things can't possibly get any worse, right?" She offered Pinky an encouraging grin, hoping to make her understand the hardest part was behind them and anything that happened at school could only pale in comparison to Mr. Michaels's reaction.

"But are you okay with…." Brynn looked down at her feet,

knuckles paling even more as she clenched the straps of her backpack. "It's me, Cassidy. I'm a 'loser', remember? Are you okay with them knowing you're with me?"

"Okay, first off, you're not a loser, so stop it. Secondly, you're just different. It's not like you're a leper or anything. You're just… unique. That's nothing to be ashamed of. I'm certainly not ash—" Cassidy's words were cut short by the sight of two senior girls walking by, holding hands and making googly eyes at one another.

Brynn's head turned, her gaze following the same girls as they passed by. For the second time that morning, they exchanged *WTF* faces. "Is it just me, or did they look like…?" Brynn queried.

"Like a couple? Yeah, totally."

"Did our school just turn into the freakin' *Twilight Zone*?"

"Who knows? Maybe we're not the only ones here—we've just been too caught up in our own stuff to realize it."

"Does that mean—" Brynn quickly looked around then leaned in. "—that we can hold hands?"

Cassidy giggled. "Do you want to hold hands? 'Cause I'm cool with any type of PDA."

"If everyone already knows…." Brynn shrugged. "And it looks like they're okay with it."

Without another word, Cassidy reached down and took Brynn's hand in hers. She smiled proudly at her girlfriend, happy that she was finally coming out of her shell. "Exactly. The worst already happened. What else could go wrong, right?"

"Oh look, now they're open about it. Someone gag me." Laura's voice came from the left of the hallway.

"I spoke too soon," Cassidy mumbled, tightening her grip on Brynn's hand and trying to control the urge to magically send Laura flying across the hall, face-first into a metal locker.

The grip Brynn had on Cassidy's hand loosened. Her sweet, innocent, shy Pinky was rocking one hell of a mean girl snarl. Her brows creased, nostrils flared. Her lips were pursed and her jaw tight. She stomped her way across the hall and stood nose to nose with the girl she'd once called a best friend.

"You listen right now, and you listen well," Brynn said.

Cassidy's eyes widened. She couldn't make herself look away, like spotting a train wreck and waiting for the bodies to be pulled out of the carnage. Laura looked terrified. Her face paled as Brynn stabbed her finger at Laura's sternum.

"You're really starting to piss me off," Brynn said. "We were best friends, and you got mad because someone else came into my life. Get. Over. It. If you would find yourself a boyfriend or... or girlfriend... or whatever, you wouldn't be so jealous of me and Cassidy. Now, you can either deal with it or drop dead, but you're *going* to leave us alone. Got it?"

Laura didn't so much as open her mouth. She stared at Brynn. Everyone around them stared at the two of them. Cassidy smirked. Her little Pinky wasn't so shy anymore. And Cassidy wanted to applaud her for it.

She felt magic crackle through every cell in her body. Sparks of energy begged to be released. Instead of making Laura slam into a locker, she channeled all that power into the source of her pride, Brynn. Walking to stand at her side, she held Brynn's hand while a few people gathered around them applauded. Some cheered. Others snickered at the way Laura tucked tail and ducked down, slipping away from in front of Brynn before booking it down the hallway and disappearing into the mass of bodies.

"I'm proud of you," Cassidy said lovingly.

"I have no idea where that came from, but it felt... a-freaking-mazing."

"Because you finally took a stand against a witch."

"I thought I was standing *with* a witch," Brynn teased, giving Cassidy a playful wink.

"I'm like the good witch… only I dress better, and you can't tell anyone about my pointy hat."

"Never. I wouldn't out you like that."

"I know." Cassidy smiled. "Now, can we officially declare that nothing else can go wrong to—"

Brynn immediately reached up and clamped her hand over Cassidy's mouth. She shook her head and said, "Not another word. Your mouth keeps getting us in trouble."

Cassidy moved Brynn's hand away to reveal a wicked grin. "I thought you liked the trouble my mouth gets you into."

"Hmmm." Brynn's head waffled from side to side. "Sometimes. Okay, most of the time." She laughed. "We're going to get in even more trouble if we don't get to class."

"Ugh, class. Okay, I'll see you later, yeah?"

"Totally," Brynn said, then she spun on her heels and headed down the hall. Cassidy watched every step she took, even after Brynn looked back and caught her watching. She couldn't possibly be the only one around to notice that for the first time since spotting Brynn Michaels, the emo girl walked with a spring in her step and her head held high, daring the world.

It was a magical sight.

Chapter 33

THE next day at school went much the same as their first day back after Brynn's disastrous coming out with her parents. One of the drama-club boys actually looked at her and said, "Baby, you were born this way," winked, then skipped off. Brynn didn't exactly know how to respond to that. Despite detesting every Lady Gaga song *ever*, she got it. That song had turned into the theme for every gay kid across the planet, apparently.

Whatever. At least they weren't teasing her. And the ironic part, Cassidy's friends even welcomed her into the fold. She was hanging with the popular kids now... pink hair and all. Her only regret was that Laura still hadn't spoken to her, and it sincerely looked like her best friend was... well, not.

"Cassidy, hurry!" she called across the parking lot.

Cassidy was stuck talking it up with their cheer coach, and the clock quickly ticked down the minutes. If they didn't get home soon, Brynn would miss the chance to see her mom before Nana, Mrs. Rivers, and her mother all headed to the PFLAG meeting. She really wanted to see her mom. Sure, it'd only been two days, but she was used to talking to her mother every single evening after school.

When Brynn saw Cassidy wave to the coach, then push through the gate, her heart started beating a little faster. She got a little more antsy. She loved Cassidy to pieces, but OMG she needed to hurry!

"I'm sorry," Cassidy called out, shuffling faster toward Brynn. "We were talking about regionals and who's gonna be the captain next year. The junior varsity girls are all two left feet!" She dug her keys from her designer handbag and jingled them in the air as she finally neared the car. "I know you wanna see your mom."

"Yes. I do. I haven't seen her since Tuesday, and if we don't hurry, we'll miss them."

"So quit standing there and get in the car, silly."

The alarm chirped and the lights flickered on just before Cassidy opened the door, tossed her stuff in the back, and slid in behind the wheel.

Brynn climbed into the car and set her backpack down between her legs. She tried to be patient, but that just wasn't going to happen. Even as Cassidy pulled out of the school parking lot, Brynn silently prayed for her to go faster.

Her sporty little car wound around the corners. Cassidy sped, but not too much, not enough to get her in trouble, and the powers that be must've been watching, because every single light turned green as they approached. They pulled down into the neighborhood just in time to catch the three women stepping out of the front door of the Riverses' home.

"Oh! Hurry!" Brynn bounced excitedly.

"I'm hurrying. I'm hurrying."

Cassidy parked behind Brynn's mom's minivan and barely had the car in park before Brynn bounded out the door. "Mom! Wait!"

Brynn's mom stopped and smiled. She held out her arms as Brynn charged toward her. "I was hoping to see you before we left. How was school?"

"Laura told everyone about me and Cassidy," Brynn panted. "But it's cool. Everyone was cool with it. The cheerleaders are actually being nice to me."

"Well, that's good." Brynn's mom hugged her tight, then released her. "We have to go, but I brought pizza from that place on the square you love so much. We'll be gone a few hours, but I would love to see you when we get back, if you're still up."

"I will be. I promise."

"Good."

She kissed Brynn's forehead and wished her daughter a good night, then climbed into the back of Mrs. Rivers's car. Brynn watched as they pulled away, wishing they'd gotten there an hour earlier just so she could hang with her mom for a bit. When she'd lived at home, she'd hated when her mom had called her into the kitchen for their afternoon talks, but now, she missed it.

With a sigh, she turned back to Cassidy, who was waiting at the top of the driveway. She put on her best smile and headed up to join her girlfriend.

"Did I hear something about pizza?" Cassidy asked as she walked to the front door.

"Yeah, my mom bought us pizza from one of my favorite places. She wants me awake when she gets back. You feel like staying up with me?"

"Sure." Cassidy smiled. "I have homework to do and some routines to work on for the junior varsity team, so I'll be up for a while. Wanna watch a movie or something after we get stuff done?"

"That sounds great."

But the moment they headed into the living room where they spent their evenings on studies and random silliness, Brynn heard a knock at the front door. She looked back at Cassidy and frowned. Her girlfriend shrugged.

They both went back to the door to find none other than Brynn's ex-best friend standing there with a fake smile plastered to her face. Brynn and Cassidy exchanged a quick glance, but it was Cassidy who said, "What are you doing here? What do you want?"

"I thought I could talk to my friend without her guard dog attacking me," Laura said.

"I'm sorry, cow, but you don't have any friends. Certainly not inside *this* house."

Laura opened her mouth, but Brynn stepped between the two of them and pushed them back before they had a chance to rip each other's heads off. "Stop it, you two." She gave Cassidy a *please behave* look, then turned back to Laura. "Seriously, though, what do you want?"

"My boyfriend said I should apologize to you, so here I am."

"Well, that's real…. Wait—" Brynn frowned. "Since when do you have a boyfriend?"

Cassidy snorted. "Boyfriend. I wasn't aware Satan took on girlfriends, but whateverrrr. I'm gonna go start on my homework." She turned to Brynn and kissed her cheek before wiggling her fingers in a wave at Laura. "Poor sap. Give him my condolences." And with that, Brynn's girlfriend disappeared into the house.

Brynn sighed and shook her head. Apparently, the two of them would never, ever get along. Not that Brynn really expected them to. Some people were never meant to be aware of each other's existence.

"Like I was saying." Brynn looked back at Laura, who was still glaring in Cassidy's general direction.

"Since you ditched me for the popular kids," Laura all but pouted. "It's been a few weeks."

"Who is it?"

"Norman Fletcher."

"Nerdy Norman?" Brynn gasped. Laura flinched. "Sorry."

"Yeah, like, don't call him that, and I won't talk about your prissy, vapid girlfriend."

"Look, if you came here to call names—"

"I didn't. Anyway, Norman said I should apologize for being so hateful to you. And honestly—" Laura took a deep breath, then slowly exhaled. "—I agree with him. It was really nasty of me to tell your parents about you, but I was hurt, so I lashed out. I had to get you back for being so… whatever with me."

"You have no idea what that did to me, Laura."

"Yeah, I kinda do." Laura stuffed her hands in the pockets of her hoodie and shrugged. Apparently, she wouldn't be looking directly at Brynn again, because her stare ping-ponged all over the place, and she never really looked Brynn in the eyes. "Anyway, like I said, I'm sorry. I wish I could take it back, but I can't. And you probably hate me now so—"

"I don't hate you."

"I would if I were you," Laura mumbled.

"Maybe I'm just a better person than you are," Brynn blurted, but the moment she said it, she wished she could take it back. "I'm so sorry," she said, eyes wide, hand hovering over her mouth. "I didn't mean that."

"I deserved it. I did something really horrible to you, and it wasn't fair. But, Brynn, you really hurt my feelings. We were supposed to be best friends. You're all I had."

"We can still be friends."

"No, we really can't. Your girlfriend hates my guts. I'll never be part of her... *your* crowd. I just wanted to say I was sorry, not beg for you to be my friend again."

"Well, I forgive you."

"Good. I, um—" Laura thumbed over her shoulder. "—guess I'm going to go now. I'll, um, see you around."

"Yeah. Sure." Brynn nodded.

Brynn didn't close the door until Laura was in her car heading out of the neighborhood. Honestly, she didn't trust Laura not to turn that apology into some kind of horrible prank. That's the moment when Brynn knew beyond a shadow of a doubt their friendship had truly ended—no do-overs, no second chances... over.

After closing that chapter of her life by accepting the fact things would never be the same with Laura, she went back to the girl who had become her best friend, who'd proven herself in more ways than Brynn could recount. When she found Cassidy sitting on the living room floor with a box of pizza on the table next to her book, Brynn kneeled down beside her and laid her head on Cassidy's shoulder. She said a soft, "I love you."

"I love you too. Is everything okay with Gothzilla?"

"I believe we just said our good-byes to each other. But she's sorry for everything she did."

"Well, at least there's that. I'm kinda sorry you lost a friend, though. That part sorta sucks, regardless of how psycho she is."

"She wasn't always like that, though." Brynn untucked her legs from beneath her so she could sit down on the floor. She reached across the table and grabbed a slice of now lukewarm pizza. "She used to be the only person who would talk to me."

"Exactly. Psycho." Cassidy laughed and nudged her shoulder against Brynn's playfully, knocking the pizza slightly away from her mouth, causing it to hit her cheek.

"Gee thanks. Now I have pizza sauce on my face." Brynn huffed. "Hand me a napkin, please."

"What are you talking about?" Cassidy leaned down and swiped her tongue across Brynn's cheek, cleaning up the sauce as she giggled. "You're nuts. There isn't anything there."

"Oh, I guess you got it." Brynn lifted the pizza to her lips, but at the last second dipped her finger in the cheese and pulled back an impressive glob of sauce. She ran it down Cassidy's cheek and smirked.

Clearly, Cassidy was well prepared, because she simply smirked back and said, "You gonna clean that before it drips down onto my designer shirt?"

Heat shot through Brynn's cheek. While she knew her tongue would soon be lapping across Cassidy's face, there was so much more she wanted to do, and it all included having them both naked. She swallowed hard, then pressed her lips to Cassidy's cheek and slowly kissed away the sauce.

"That's hella better than the napkin I was expecting you to use…."

"I figured *that's* what you expected me to do."

"Oh my little emo bunny, you're full of surprises lately." Cassidy laughed as she reached for a few napkins. She handed one over to Brynn, then swiped another across her own cheek to clear off whatever might be left.

Brynn shrugged as she cleaned her cheek as well. "I guess I feel... I don't know... more like 'me' now. Like I'm being real or something."

Cassidy set her pen down into the crease of her open book. She shifted her weight slightly, bringing her face to face with Brynn. The smile gracing her flawless features was a sight Brynn knew she wouldn't grow tired of anytime soon, if ever at all. "I feel the same way. Before you came around, I was super popular but no one ever really knew *me,* ya know? Somehow, you snuck under all my defenses and walls, and before I knew it, I didn't want to keep anything from you. For a girl who's always hidden behind a designer outfit and a holier-than-thou attitude, that's a lot. So, um... thanks, I guess. For giving me a chance regardless of what you saw."

"God, if you could've seen you through my eyes," Brynn whispered, lowering her gaze.

"Believe me, I know what I seemed like. It was all done on purpose. You saw past it all anyway. It was like—" The brilliant smile lit up Cassidy's cobalt gaze. "—like magic. I'm the witch, but you're the real magical one, Brynnie."

Nothing Brynn could say would possibly top that, and yet she felt the urge to blurt out every ridiculous rambling thought in her brain. So before she made an utter fool out of herself, she closed her eyes and claimed Cassidy's lips. That was a hell of a lot better than going on about everything and anything, and holy crap, Cassidy's lips still tasted like strawberries... even with the pizza.

Epilogue

"SAY cheese!" Cassidy's mother held a camera up to her face as Nana posed Brynn and Cassidy in yet another exaggerated embrace at the base of the stairs.

"Mom, don't you think you have enough pictures?"

Nana gasped. "We can never have enough pictures of your prom night! This is wonderful!"

"It is kinda epic," Brynn chimed in, smiling.

She looked radiant. Even though she wore a black strapless gown, the color didn't dull her shine. A series of thin, silver necklaces accentuated her collarbone, dropping in different lengths across the front of the satiny dress, all the way down to the empire cut. She'd dyed her hair a few shades brighter. Where it was usually cotton-candy-colored, it was now shiny, bright hot pink, and made an amazing contrast against her pale skin and dark dress. Cassidy was shamelessly ogling her—again, when Nana cleared her throat.

"Well, I don't know about epic. In my days, *The Iliad* was epic. But this only happens once in your lives, so pipe down, Cassidy, and let your mom capture every detail of the moment."

"Yes, Nana." Cassidy shut up and wrapped her corsaged arm around Brynn's small waist just like her grandmother insisted.

Admittedly, they looked amazing. Cassidy had chosen a vintage white Vera Wang cocktail dress that tapered off one shoulder and ended in a mock tuxedo cut in the rear. Her shapely legs looked killer in the matching heels, complete with rhinestone bows above the peep toes. When they'd first come down, Brynn had joked and said they looked like bride and groom at an altar, but despite the contrasts, they really did make a very pretty couple.

"Great, now turn to the side, and Brynn, wrap your arms around Cassidy's waist," Nana, the professional prom-picture-stager-person, demanded. But before the girls could strike another pose, there was a knock at the door.

"I think that might be my mom," Brynn said, her tone joyous. It meant a lot to her that her mother said she'd come down to see her off before the limo picked them up for their big night.

Brynn hopped down from the bottom step before another picture could be taken. She practically bounced all the way to the door. Even though Cassidy saw her get that excited every time her mother came to visit them, the absolute thrill it gave Brynn made her smile. It made those little happy butterflies flitter beneath Cassidy's skin.

Since Brynn still lived with them, her mother only came to visit once a month when she had PFLAG meetings with Nana and Cassidy's mother, or if she happened to sneak away for something. Unfortunately, Brynn's father hadn't come around yet, and it was starting to look like he never would. Sad.

She watched as Pinky turned the knob and pulled the door open, and what she saw made every person in the room come to a dead stop. She even gasped.

Brynn's dad stood just in front of her mother. Frankly, the man looked like he'd been through hell. It had been a little over three months since he'd kicked Brynn out of their house, and truth be told, it really didn't look like the man had slept a wink since. His eyes were dark, bags hanging heavy beneath them. His five o'clock shadow had a five o'clock shadow. He looked just... bad.

"Brynn," he said. His voice was hoarse, as if he'd spent the better part of a day fighting not to cry. He cleared his throat. "You look beautiful."

"Daddy?" she breathed. "What are you... doing here?"

"I had to see my little girl off to her prom."

Cassidy could see Brynn's shoulders square, as if she'd inhaled or maybe she was fighting to keep upright and not fling herself at her father. And one of the things Cassidy had honed over the months was her ability to see auras. She'd come to learn when Brynn was her happiest, her aura shimmered and became more vibrant. When her Pinky worried or became nervous, her aura darkened. Never once had she seen Brynn's aura dim like it did the moment she saw her father. Even the room seemed to chill.

"I'm going with Cassidy," she said with a lot more resolve than Cassidy ever expected from her. Brynn hiked her hands up to her hips and glanced over her shoulder. Hopefully, she saw Cassidy's pleased smile.

"I know," he said. "I expected you to."

"And you're not mad?"

"Honey," he said, "Your mom has taught me a lot... not to mention those pamphlets I've been mysteriously receiving in the mail for the past two months."

Every head in the room turned to Nana.

"What?" She shrugged. "Didn't we have more pictures to take?"

"Mom!" Cassidy's mother exclaimed.

"Who said I did it?"

"Nana, c'mon. You've got more LGBT lit hiding around this house than anyone I've ever seen."

Since Nana had decided to help jump-start the PFLAG chapter and youth group in Majestic Hills, the stuff had been arriving in boxes on almost a daily basis. Thankfully, Nana had bought her own place in the neighborhood, so Cassidy was slowly gaining the space in her room back.

"Well," Mr. Michaels said. "If your Nana is to blame for it, I thank her."

"In that case," Nana said. "Yes, it was me."

Cassidy and her mother both shook their heads.

"It helped. I didn't know a lot of those things. The facts were... well, convincing. Anyway, I didn't want my little girl hurting anymore. I know this life isn't going to be easy, and frankly, it scared me. I don't want you to be bullied, and I don't want people judging you for loving another girl."

"Daddy, you have to trust that I'm strong enough to handle it. I'm a big girl now."

"All grown-up. I can see." Mr. Michaels held out his arms. "Can my grown-up give me a hug?"

"Of course," Brynn said as she stepped into her father's arms. Behind them, her mother wiped tears from her eyes. They were happy tears, that was clear by the smile curling her pink lips. Even Cassidy had to fight back her own tears.

"Okay, I want pictures before there isn't a dry eye in the place," Nana declared.

A chorus of laughter erupted, and the chill that had once filled the living room dispelled and calm warmth rolled through. Everything was finally as it should be. Pinky was happy again, genuinely happy. Her joy showed in the sparkle of her eyes and in the way her smile pushed those precious dimples into her cheeks. It radiated in the glow of her skin and the bright, vibrant shimmer of her aura.

And Cassidy couldn't be happier than she was in that moment, simply because Brynn finally had her peace.

"Okay, line up at the staircase," Nana said as she waved everyone over.

Mr. and Mrs. Michaels stood at either side of Brynn. Nana, Cassidy, and her mother all stood back and watched the reunited family revel in their togetherness, and just before Nana snapped off another picture, Brynn's father said, "Cassidy, why don't you join us."

Before Cassidy could reply, her mother spoke up for her. "She'd love to," Miranda said, gently giving Cassidy a push from behind. Cassidy hesitated at first, but Brynn's hopeful stare cut through her reluctance. She slowly made her way over, where Brynn's mother made space in between her and her daughter so Cassidy could fit in.

"What a lovely picture!" Nana said happily. "The portrait of a young, LGBT-accepting family. I might be able to use this for one of our PFLAG brochures."

"Well, hold on just a moment there...," Brynn's dad spoke up, voice uncertain and not a little uncomfortable.

"She's kidding, dear. She does that a lot," Cassidy heard Brynn's mother whisper behind her.

"Oh. Of course."

They spent a few more minutes posing for pictures, some with just Brynn and her parents, others with Cassidy, Nana, and her mom. Brynn suggested setting up the camera's timer and tripod so they could have a snapshot of everyone together, and that took about fifteen minutes. Either Nana set the tricky timer wrong and the camera caught them unready or someone smiled goofily, got caught close-eyed, and one time they even got caught bustling to stand in place, resulting in nothing more than blurry bodies in the shot. Finally—at about the seventh take—they managed to produce a beautiful family portrait.

Just in time, too, because the moment they all agreed the picture was finally perfect, the limousine Cassidy's mom had hired for the night beeped the horn outside.

"They're here!" Cassidy exclaimed excitedly.

Everyone scrambled into "go" mode. Nana rushed to grab the clutch purses the girls had picked out. Brynn's mother and father hugged Brynn, reminding her to be safe and to call them in case of any emergencies, and Miranda stood in front of Cassidy, smiling as a well of unshed tears brimmed her lashes.

"I'm so proud of you, Cassidy. You've grown into such an

independent, freethinking young woman. Have fun tonight, sweetheart. You deserve it." She pressed a kiss to Cassidy's cheek, and then turned to Brynn as she approached the door. "You too, Brynn. You look absolutely beautiful tonight. Have fun, honey."

"Thanks, Miranda."

"Thanks, Mom."

Brynn and Cassidy spoke in unison. They laced their fingers together and headed out to the dusky evening, where the sleek, black limo waited at the curb, complete with a white-gloved driver standing at attention, holding the door open for them.

"Good evening, ladies."

Again, in unison, they both greeted him and entered the confines of the limo's plush backseat. Inside, they were greeted by Leah, Jenna, Tara, Michelle, Sandy, and her date, Eric, all cheerleaders—minus Eric—who had become good friends with Brynn over the past few months.

It turned out that Tara and Michelle discovered they were also into girls. Well, they discovered they were into each other, and that led them to figure out their sexuality. Leah's boyfriend was in college so he couldn't go to the prom, and Jenna was happily single. Sandy and Eric had been dating since freshman year, so they were happy to have survived the four levels of hell to celebrate that night.

Much to poor Eric's obvious dismay, the ride to the hotel where the prom was being hosted was spent talking about dresses, shoes, and corsages and the predicted prom king and queen, who everyone swore would be Cassidy and Zeden Scott, the captain of the football team.

Since the nomination rumors started swirling a month before the prom tickets even went on sale, Cassidy had repeatedly assured Brynn that she and Zeden had been friends since elementary school, and there wasn't anything *at all* between them. However, Brynn's lips still pursed together at the mention of her girlfriend dancing with a jock or, really, any time Cassidy's and Zeden's names were mentioned in the same sentence.

Nothing changed now. Brynn sat up with all but a scowl on her pretty lips.

"Brynnie, it's tradition," Tara offered, smiling softly at Brynn.

"Yeah, Brynn. I'm sure Zeden's girlfriend would love to rip the crown off Cassidy's head, ya know?" Michelle laughed.

Cassidy scoffed. "As if that troll could even reach my head. She's, like, four feet nothing."

"Brynn, if it makes you feel better, I'll dance with you while Cassidy and Zeden are dancing." Eric winked, then shrieked as Sandy stomped on his foot.

"Who will *I* dance with then?" she demanded, a playful pout on her face.

"Nah, it's cool," Brynn said, taking Cassidy's hand in hers. "I just hope they don't pick some cheesy love song for them to dance to."

"Oh my gawd, I'd refuse!" Cassidy gasped.

They all laughed and kept talking, and before they knew it, the limo slowed down and came to a stop in front of the hotel's luxurious, palm-tree-lined entrance. The driver opened the door, and all the girls scrambled out, with Eric catching up from the rear.

Inside the hotel lobby, they gave their tickets at the table and signed their names in the guest book. Natasha Ramsey, the junior in charge of the welcome committee, informed them that they were taking complimentary pictures to the left of the ballroom entrance. Cassidy was eager to get inside, but at Brynn's request for an official picture, she followed behind her girlfriend to the small roped-off section the school had designated as the photo area. There, at the end of the short line, stood Laura with her nerdy boyfriend, Norman.

Over the months, Brynn and Laura had slowly begun talking again. They weren't as close as they once were, but they recently reached the point where all four of them went out on a double date to the movies. Cassidy was far from being Laura's BFF, and Laura wasn't making shopping dates with her any time soon, but they were friendly to each other for Brynn's sake. Cassidy knew her efforts were something Pinky appreciated, so she fought back the commentary about Laura's green dress resembling baby vomit as they came to stand behind the now brunette Laura and Norman, whose tie matched Laura's dress.

"Hey, you two look great," Brynn said, smiling brightly as she tapped Laura on the shoulder.

She spun around and offered Brynn an equally bright smile. "Oh, thanks!"

Norman turned around, smiled, and commented on how pretty their dresses were.

When it was their turn to take pictures, Norman suggested they all take a picture together. Cassidy obliged, standing next to Brynn while Norman and Laura stood to their left in a picturesque embrace. Laura and Brynn took a picture together, and finally, each couple posed for their official prom photo.

"See you inside," Laura said cheerfully before taking her boyfriend and tugging him along toward the entrance.

Cassidy followed suit and took Brynn's hand, escorting her to the double doors of the ballroom. Inside, the theme was "Once Upon a Fairy Tale." They had to walk down a white carpet leading through the center of two rows of artificial trees with branches intertwined above. It resembled an enchanted forest, complete with blue, white, and silver balloons as the trees' magical shrubbery.

Once they passed through the "forest," everything was covered in glitter. The room sparkled from the rapid pulsing lights flashing in rhythm with the upbeat dance music pouring through the massive speakers set up everywhere. Columns set up to resemble fairy tale castle pillars gave way to a dance floor surrounded by white linen-covered tables, accented by chairs wrapped with satiny blue bows. Strips of sheer fabric hung along the walls, backlit by strings of twinkling Christmas lights. Shimmering stars hung from the ceiling at various lengths.

"Wow, this is—" Brynn gasped as she looked around.

"Magical?" Cassidy laughed. "That was kinda my route when pitching themes to the committee. I may or may not have stressed this idea the most."

"As always, you've outdone yourself, Cassidy."

"Thank you, but the credit goes to my muse."

"I hear she's pretty awesome," Brynn said, grinning.

"She's more than awesome. She rocks my world."

"Quit being a sap in front of all these people."

"Baby, you've not seen sappy yet." Cassidy smirked and took Brynn's hand, leading her to the dance floor, where the fast tempo of the music slowed down and Eve 6's "Here's To The Night" started to play, almost as if on cue for them.

Brynn pressed close to her body as they began to sway in time with the song. Laura and Norman danced to their left. Tara and Michelle walked out, also to embrace one another as they danced.

There, surrounded by friends and the magic of the moment, with the girl she loved more than anything dancing with her, Cassidy couldn't care less about the crown or attention that came with being a prom queen. She had all she needed right there, in an emo black dress and hot pink hair. And that was better than anything else she could be awarded.

ZOE LYNNE strives to give LGBT youth stories they love, with heroes they can relate to. Zoe Lynne began in October of 2012, with the sole focus being to create books with LGBT youth in mind. It is Zoe Lynne's hope to deliver characters who are both real and fantastic, characters you love and love to hate, but more so, characters you can relate to. The author behind Zoe Lynne has received accolades in adult romance.

Find more from Zoe Lynne at http://zoelynnebooks.blogspot.com or follow on Facebook: https://www.facebook.com/ZoeLynneBooks.

Also from HARMONY INK PRESS

SARA GAINES

NOBLE
FALLING

http://www.harmonyinkpress.com

Fantasy from HARMONY INK PRESS

HALLIE BURTON

tapestry

http://www.harmonyinkpress.com

Harmony Ink

CPSIA information can be obtained at www.ICGtesting.com
Printed in the USA
LVOW05s1517100214

373092LV00003B/673/P

9 781623 809270